This was the biggest ~~~ of her life.

She had practically s~~~ ~~~ soul to spend one sizzling night with a man who had reinvented the word *satisfaction*.

Lying together now, front to naked front, Veda studied the cocky cowboy in question. Whenever his lips twitched with a nocturnal grin, her insides squeezed, begging for just one more kiss.

Just one more time.

Damn it, she knew better.

Still asleep, Ajax Rawson drew in a sharp breath at the same time his grip on her flexed and then dug in more. Veda had to bite her lip to stem the groan; her Benedict Arnold body wanted those expert hands everywhere and all at once. And if he woke up now, that could very well be where they'd end up.

Making love like nothing else mattered.

As if there weren't already enough prices to pay.

* * *

One Night with His Rival by Robyn Grady
is part of the About That Night... series.

Dear Reader,

You're in for one heck of a ride!

If you've read my previous Desire release, *The Case for Temptation*—where media heiress Teagan Hunter finally gets her very own happily-ever-after—you'll be familiar with Ajax Rawson, the scrumptious, laid-back boss at the Rawson Stud Farm. Whether he's mixing with fellow New York State elite or rocking a pair of low-riding jeans at his stables, Ajax loves what he does...and that includes playing the field. Life doesn't get any better than that.

Then he meets Veda Darnel and his "living the dream" existence is turned on its head.

Since her teens, Veda has crushed on Ajax Rawson from afar. After a scorching one-night stand, she can't believe fantasy is now bone-melting reality. However, as delectable as this guy is—particularly in bed—the notion of a second helping is off the table. Forget the fact that her father loathes the Rawsons, and Ajax's lady-killer reputation is legendary. There's a massive scandal brewing, which, along with a closely guarded secret, cancels out any chance of this fling becoming more. No matter how much Ajax tries to seduce her again—and, boy oh boy, does he try!—Veda must stay strong and get this sweet-talking cowboy out of her life.

Twists and turns laced with plenty of sizzle... Don't forget to buckle up before you enjoy *One Night with His Rival*!

Best wishes and happy reading,

Robyn

www.RobynGrady.com

@robyngrady

ROBYN GRADY

ONE NIGHT WITH HIS RIVAL

HARLEQUIN

DESIRE

HARLEQUIN®
DESIRE™

ISBN-13: 978-1-335-20899-6

One Night with His Rival

Copyright © 2020 by Robyn Grady

Recycling programs
for this product may
not exist in your area.

This edition published by arrangement with Harlequin Books S.A.

For questions and comments about the quality of this book,
please contact us at CustomerService@Harlequin.com.

Harlequin Enterprises ULC
22 Adelaide St. West, 40th Floor
Toronto, Ontario M5H 4E3, Canada
www.Harlequin.com

Printed in U.S.A.

Robyn Grady was first contracted by Harlequin in 2006. Her books feature regularly on bestseller lists and at award ceremonies, including the National Readers' Choice Awards, Booksellers' Best Awards, CataRomance Reviewers' Choice Awards and Australia's prestigious Romantic Book of the Year.

Robyn lives on Australia's gorgeous Sunshine Coast, where she met and married her real-life hero. When she's not tapping out her next story, she enjoys the challenges of raising three very different daughters, going to the theater, reading on the beach and dreaming about bumping into Stephen King during a month-long Mediterranean cruise.

Robyn knows that writing romance is the best job on the planet and she loves to hear from her readers! You can keep up with news on her latest releases at www.robyngrady.com.

Books by Robyn Grady

Harlequin Desire

About That Night...

The Case for Temptation
One Night with His Rival

Visit her Author Profile page at Harlequin.com, or robyngrady.com, for more titles.

You can also find Robyn Grady on Facebook, along with other Harlequin Desire authors, at www.Facebook.com/HarlequinDesireAuthors!

With thanks to my wonderful editor,
Charles Griemsman, and literary agent
extraordinaire, Jessica Alvarez.
Professional, supportive and talented.
I just love working with you both.

One

Last night was the best and worst decision of her life. On the one hand, it was ecstasy. On the other hand, disaster.

Veda Darnel couldn't get her head around it. She had practically sold her soul to spend one sizzling night with a man who had reinvented the word *satisfaction*. A consummate charmer who'd caused her to swap out her common sense for the thrill of unparalleled pleasure.

Lying together now, front to naked front, Veda studied the cocky cowboy in question as he continued to grab some much-needed sleep. Primal instinct was keeping his hand glued to her behind, pressing her hips against his. Each time he breathed in, that mouth-watering chest expanded and wiry hairs teased her nipples. Whenever his lips twitched with a dream-induced grin, she longed for just one more kiss.

Just one more time.

Well, sorry, universe. Not happening. Not now. Not ever again. Damn it, she knew better. In the future, would *do* better.

Still asleep, Ajax Rawson drew in a sharp breath at the same time the fingers on her butt flexed, then dug in more. Veda had to bite her lip to stem the groan; her Benedict Arnold body wanted those expert hands everywhere and all at once. And if he woke up now, that could very well be where they'd end up. Making love like nothing else mattered.

As if there weren't already enough prices to pay.

Tippy-toe quiet, she reached behind her and found the big, hot hand cupping her rear end. She carefully coiled her fingers around his wrist, then tried to lift and shift it.

Seriously? His arm must be made of lead.

Knuckling down, Veda tried again. When she'd finally managed to ease herself away, she held her breath. But he didn't stir. Not an inch.

So, slide off the bed, dive into your clothes, bolt out the hotel suite's front door and never look back. Never go back. Still, a knot of bittersweet longing kept her hanging. Ajax was the best she'd ever had—the best there ever was.

And how many other women had thought the exact same thing?

He sucked in another sharp breath, rolled onto his back and scooped his arm under his pillow while his other hand gave those ripped abs a languid rub or two. Then his brow pinched, eyelids flickered open, and Veda's stomach dropped.

Too late to run now.

Ajax frowned sleepily at the ceiling, getting his bearings, before turning his gaze onto her. When one corner of his wholly kissable mouth eased up—when his lungs expanded on a breath that said, "Oh, yeah... I remember you"—Veda's resolve to do better wobbled like a thimble full of Jell-O.

Ajax's dreamy ocean-deep blue eyes smiled into hers as he spoke with a sexy growl that was equal parts playful and deadly serious.

"You need to come over here." He cocked an eyebrow, smiling wider as the sheet tented over his waist. "On second thought, I can't wait that long."

When he rolled back toward her, heat rushed through her blood, pooling deliciously low in her belly. But tempted as she was, Veda didn't lean in. Didn't surrender. Instead, she brought her portion of the sheet higher and sat up.

"Actually," she said, "I have to go."

Ajax paused, then leaned up on an elbow, head in hand, biceps bulging. "You mean to the bathroom or something?"

"No. Not that."

"Ah, you need food," he said. "Me, too. I'll order up. Maybe some green pepper omelets, hot-off-the-grill bacon and chocolate-chip-banana pancakes drowned in syrup. We can eat breakfast in bed." He came near enough to brush his gorgeous stubble against her cheek. "Lunch and dinner, too, if you want."

Ajax was never lost for words—more specifically, the right words. He gave off a vibe that confirmed that everything good fortune had to offer came to him naturally. Like he never had to even think about trying.

If only she could say the same for herself.

Years ago, and more than once, a much younger Veda had watched Ajax from afar while daydreaming about being in this exact situation. Back then, as well as now, she hated to think what her father might say. Drake Darnel had an ax or two to grind with the Rawsons, the first dating back decades to a time when Ajax's dad, Huxley Rawson, was known as a stud.

What was the saying?

Oh, yeah.

The apple never falls far from the tree.

Now, as Ajax maneuvered to claim that kiss—as his musky scent flooded her senses and all her pulse points started to throb—Veda felt her resistance begin to ebb. Thankfully, somehow, she managed to shore herself up and pull back in time.

Ajax pulled back, too, studying her like he couldn't work out what the problem was for the life of him. After the way she'd allowed herself to be so completely adored these past hours...really, who could blame him?

"Have I done something wrong, Veda? Have I hurt you somehow?"

She shook her head. "No. Nothing like that." He'd been a total gentleman. An incredible lover.

"Do you have somewhere else to be?"

"Not particularly, no."

His pained expression only made him look hotter, if that was even possible.

"Is this about family? About our fathers not getting along?"

She winced. "It's kind of hard to ignore."

"We did just fine ignoring it last night."

They'd met at a glitzy Saratoga Springs charity event held at a well-known venue. An hour in, needing a break from the hype, Veda had wandered out onto a balcony. Wearing a tux that fit his dynamite build to perfection, Ajax had been standing by the railing, finishing a call. Veda had swallowed her breath and promptly turned on her silver high heel. But he was already putting the phone away and asking in a rumbling voice that reduced her to mush, "Haven't we met somewhere before?"

Lamest pickup line in the playbook. Except he wasn't playing. While they had never spoken, of course she might look familiar. For years, at various horse races she'd gone to with her dad, she had been a shadow hovering in the background, fawning over Ajax.

So, had they met before?

Feeling like a tongue-tied teen again, Veda had murmured, "Not, uh, physically." Those beautiful blue eyes crinkled at the corners as he chuckled and replied, "Well then, pleased to make your acquaintance—*physically.*"

After an exchange of names, of course the penny had dropped. She was a Darnel, he was a Rawson. Veda also mentioned that she had recently become friends with Lanie Rawson, his sister. Small world…and getting smaller.

With Ajax doing most of the talking, they had gotten to know each other more. Then had come the dancing and the kissing and, after midnight, *this*. The entire time, neither one had touched on the Darnel-Rawson feud. Frankly, Veda didn't want to spoil the mesmerizing mood. Apparently Ajax hadn't given the matter a whole lot of thought.

"Drake and Hux have butted heads over the years," Ajax reflected now, "but I can't remember the last time Dad even mentioned his name."

Was he joking? "I hear my father going on about Hux Rawson all the time."

"Wait. Didn't you say you're in New Jersey now?"

He was right. She hadn't lived here in New York with her father for years. "We keep in touch…phone calls, emails. I visit when I can."

Like this weekend. In fact, she was meant to have been her father's plus-one last night. Feeling under the weather, he'd backed out at the last minute.

Way to go, fate.

"Oh. Well…" Running a hand through his delectably mussed dark blond hair, Ajax blew out a breath. "I'm sorry to hear that."

"Sorry to hear that we keep in touch?"

"Sorry that your dad hasn't moved on. Must be tough holding on to a grudge like that."

Veda's cheeks heated up more. Drake Darnel was a whole bunch of things. *But c'mon now. Let's be fair.*

"I guess it would be difficult to move on when

someone swoops in to steal the love of your life. The woman you'd planned to marry."

Ajax's tilted his cleft chin. "Did you say *steal*?"

"My father gave her a ring. Then Hux made his move and voilà." Game over.

"Uh, Drake *offered* a ring, which my mom declined. I heard that directly from her, by the way. And with regard to Dad casting some kind of a spell... Veda, it takes two to tango."

He gave the room a sweeping gaze, as if to say "case in point."

Veda wasn't finished. If they were doing this, she wanted to make the connection between then and now. Between player father and chip off the old block. Just one more reason last night had been a bad idea.

"I believe Hux had quite a reputation in those days."

Ajax frowned slightly. "He was a dude who dated before finding the right one and settling down."

Drake preferred to explain Hux's bachelor past in terms like *skirt-chaser, Casanova, cheat*, although that last dig was aimed more at the Rawsons' questionable business ethics. On top of the issue of how Hux had stolen Drake's would-be bride, the Rawsons and Darnels owned competing Thoroughbred stables. More often than not, Drake's horses were beaten by a nose by a Rawson ride.

Better training? Sporting luck? Or was something more going on behind the scenes with regard to performance?

As far as Veda was concerned, the entire horse racing industry was unethical. Cruel. That didn't even touch on the social pitfalls of gambling, where in some cases, entire paychecks were burned practically every week, leaving families in crisis. Long ago she had made a promise to herself. The day her father passed on, a for-sale sign would go up outside the front gates of the Darnel Stables and every horse would find a home without the threat of whips, injury or being shipped off to the glue factory when it was past its use-by date.

Shuddering, Veda refocused. Ajax was still talking about his folks.

"My mother and father were deeply in love. They were committed to each other and their family. Mom made a choice all those years ago. One she wouldn't hesitate to stand by if she was alive today."

Veda was sorry that Mrs. Rawson had died when Ajax was still a boy. Losing a parent at a young age changed who you were, how you coped. Every day Veda wished that her own mom was still around. She wished her childhood had been different—normal—rather than the screwup she had muddled and struggled through.

But now was not the time to go down that particular rabbit hole. She was vulnerable enough as it was.

Veda wound her hands tighter into the bedsheet she was holding close to her breasts. "I guess we'll just have to agree to disagree," she said.

"I guess we will." Ajax's gaze dropped to her lips as he added, "And if you want to leave… I get it. I do. Just please know that I don't have anything personal against your dad."

She wasn't done with being ticked off. The Rawsons had a lot to answer for. Still, Ajax's olive branch seemed so genuine, and the apologetic expression in his eyes looked so real… It wouldn't hurt to concede at least a small point.

"I don't hate your dad, either. I haven't even met the man."

"But you will. I presume Lanie invited you to her big birthday bash at home next month."

She nodded. "Should be good."

Though she wasn't looking forward to her father's reaction when he heard the news. While Drake knew that she and Lanie Rawson were more than acquaintances now, he was far from happy about it. He wouldn't care to hear that his daughter was looking forward to celebrating with her friend at her party.

And, of course, Ajax would be there, too, looking as magma-hot as he did right now.

His smile was just so easy and inviting.

"Wow. The Darnels and Rawsons finally coming together," he said. "Just goes to show, things change, huh?"

Veda gave in to a smile, too.

Just goes to show…

And because Ajax always seemed to know precisely when and exactly how to act, he chose that moment to lean in again. And when he slid that big warm hand around the back of her neck, this time Veda didn't resist. She simply closed her eyes and inwardly sighed as he pushed his fingers up through her hair and his mouth finally claimed hers the way it was always meant to. For better or worse, the way she must have wanted all along.

Two

"Eyes off. That means hands, too, partner."

Recognizing the voice at his back, Ajax edged around. Birthday girl Lanie Rawson stood there in a bright haute couture gown, hands on hips, a vigilant eyebrow raised.

Ajax played dumb. "Eyes and hands off *who* exactly?"

"If you don't already know, the bombshell you're ogling over there is Veda Darnel," his sister replied. "Drake Darnel's daughter *and* a good friend of mine."

When Ajax had gotten together with Veda four weeks ago in Saratoga, she had mentioned something about her and Lanie being tight. Frankly, in those initial few moments, he hadn't focused on anything much other than her amazing red hair and stunning lavender evening dress. Tonight, with that hair swept over one creamy shoulder and rocking a shimmering lipstick-red number, Veda looked even more heart-stopping.

Eyes off?

Never gonna happen.

Hands off?

We'll see.

Crossing his arms, Ajax rocked back on his boot heels. He'd had a full day at the stables before racing out to the track in time for the "riders up" call. After a thundering win, he'd made his way to the winner's circle to congratulate the jockey, the assistant trainer and their most recent champion, Someone's Prince Charming. Man, he loved that horse. Then he'd shot back to the on-site office to check messages and shower before driving the extra half mile here to don a tux. But first, he'd decided to take a peek at the party that was already getting under way in a glittering tented pavilion in the backyard of the estate.

Now, before he went inside to change, he had a question or two for Miss Lanie Bossy-Pants.

"How did you and Veda Darnel become pals?"

"We met at a women's business luncheon last year," Lanie explained, slipping her hands into the hidden pockets of her Cinderella gown. "Veda's a life coach. She talked about personal change through action rather than words. It was brief but powerful. Actually, I was blown away. Later, she said she recalled seeing us as kids at race meets when she tagged along with her dad. And then I remembered her, too. Or, at least, I remembered her hair."

Like the color of leaves in late fall, Ajax thought,

doing some remembering of his own, particularly images of her moving beneath him in bed that night a month ago.

"Back then," Lanie went on, "Veda was like a mouse in a corner. Now she knows exactly what she wants. And I'm pretty darn sure that doesn't include being any man's flavor of the month."

Ajax chuckled to cover up the wince. "I'm not that bad."

Lanie had a skeptical if-you-say-so expression on her face.

"Anyway, I'm glad Veda didn't buy into her father's BS about all Rawsons being scum," she said. "You know she told me once that Drake is still steaming over Mom dumping him for Dad all those years ago. Just so sad."

Sad was one word. But Ajax didn't agree with Lanie. Veda had absolutely drunk the Kool-Aid when it came to believing her father's version of events.

During their one night together, she had gone to the mat for her father. According to Daddy Dearest, Hux was a slimy villain who had stolen Drake's girl. Ajax had set the record straight. His mom had made her own decision—because, duh, it was hers to make—after which she had married the far better man.

Veda had softened toward him again after that, and before vacating their suite around noon, they'd exchanged numbers. The next day, he'd sent flowers to her Best Life Now office address in Jersey. After a week not hearing from her, he'd called and left a message. A few days later, he'd sent a bigger bunch. Dialed again.

No response.

"She's smart, tough and to the point," Lanie said, looking Veda's way through the glittering party crowd. "Not someone who's desperate for a roll in the hay."

When Lanie pinned him with another look that said, *Don't go there*, Ajax coughed out a laugh. "You're seriously the sex police now?"

His sister tossed back her long dark hair the way she did whenever she was excited, angry or digging her spurs in. "I want to make sure that we're clear before I let you out to graze."

He threw her a salute. "Anything you say, Officer."

Lanie groaned. "Just go get changed. Not that the ladies won't drool over you in your boots." Walking off, his sister offered a fond grin when she added, "You're such a tart."

After parking in the designated area out in front of the Rawson property, Veda had followed a torchlit path that wove around the majestic Victorian mansion to a tent filled with conversation and music. She'd been taking in the swagged ceilings, which were awash with a million fairy lights, and looking out for anyone she might know when, larger than life, Ajax appeared at the entrance.

With hands bracing either side of his belt, Ajax was wearing a white business shirt rolled up enough at the sleeves to reveal his strong, tanned forearms. A sexy five-o'clock shadow highlighted the natural thrust of his jaw and cleft chin. Even from this distance, even in this light, his eyes radiated a hue that brought to mind ocean-deep waters sparkling with midsummer sunshine.

Following that whirlwind night in Saratoga, he'd sent two enormous bouquets of flowers. Both times when he called, Veda had ached to pick up. At some stage tonight, they were destined to run into each other. When they did, would Ajax try to reconnect? Were any sparks left on his side of the equation, or after her snub, was she already a speck in Ajax Rawson's rearview mirror?

Before he'd been able to spot her, Veda had inserted herself into a nearby circle of guests. Now she sneaked another look his way.

Lanie had joined him; given his sister's expression, their discussion wasn't particularly lighthearted. When Lanie walked off, Ajax left and Veda released a pent-up breath. She was safe—at least for now. Then Lanie headed Veda's way, which raised another question.

She and Lanie hadn't been in touch for weeks. Had Ajax mentioned anything to his sister about Saratoga? Lanie knew Veda wasn't the type to fall into bed with a guy for the heck of it. But after years of wondering, she had taken the opportunity to at last scratch her Ajax Rawson itch. And as much as she tried—as much as she knew she probably should—Veda couldn't regret a moment of the amazing time they had spent together.

When Lanie was a few feet away, she was joined by a man Veda recognized. Hux Rawson was tall and broad through the shoulders like his son, with neat steel-gray hair, complete with a widow's peak. He dropped a kiss on his daughter's cheek before he hooked an arm through hers and escorted Lanie on her way.

Right toward Veda.

Her head began to spin. From the way Lanie had described her dad, Hux would be gracious, even in welcoming Drake Darnel's daughter. In similar circumstances, she doubted her father would be as polite. Although he was aware that she and Lanie were friends now, Drake still disapproved of all the Rawsons. Always had.

Always would.

Red carpet ready in a tiered canary-yellow tulle gown and smelling like rose petals, Lanie gave Veda a hug and exclaimed, "You look positively gorgeous."

Veda was never good with compliments, so she simply passed on her best wishes, adding, "I left something on the gift table."

A glossy hard copy of the history of women in equestrian sports. Nothing Veda would ever want herself, but coming across it in a Princeton bookstore, she had known dressage champion Lanie would love it.

Lanie saw to introductions. "Veda Darnel, meet the most important man in my life."

An easy smile lit her father's bright blue eyes. "Glad you could make it, Veda. I'm Hux."

For a man in his midsixties, Hux Rawson cut a fine figure in his pristine tuxedo. The tanned face and smile lines bracketing his mouth suggested a long run of good health and personal happiness. Veda's father only ever looked annoyed—unless he was in his stables.

Nothing against the horses, but there was more to life than work and stewing over the past.

Tacking up a smile, Veda replied, "It's great to be here."

"Hard to believe my little girl is twenty-seven today." Hux gave his daughter a wink. "So beautiful *and* conquering the world."

Lanie pretended to wither. "Pressure much?"

"You know I'm proud of you," Hux said, obviously referring to more than her riding achievements. "I know your mother would be proud of you, too."

Lanie's expression softened before something over her dad's shoulder caught her eye. Bouncing up on her toes, she signaled to a couple entering the tent.

"Will you two excuse me?" She snatched a champagne flute from a passing waiter's tray. "A hostess's job is never done."

Hux smiled as he watched his daughter hurry off, then returned his attention to Veda. There was a moment of uncertainty about kicking off the conversation again, which wasn't uncommon between newly introduced people. Except this man wasn't exactly a stranger. His decisions before Veda was even born had affected her life on so many levels, in ways he couldn't possibly know—in ways that could still leave her feeling a little lost.

Like now.

Looking directly into her eyes, feeling the weight of the past pressing in…

She wasn't surprised when a chill scuttled up her spine, then slithered around her throat—and squeezed.

The sensation wasn't new. It went back as far as elementary school when she had tried to learn her letters; they looked more like squiggling tadpoles in a white sea, no matter what her teacher had said. In later grades, whenever she was pushed to read in class or was feeling stressed, her ears would begin to ring and her throat would close. Feeling everyone's eyes on her, she would literally freeze, unable to speak. Whispers and open snipes followed her everywhere, even in her dreams.

Lazy.

Dumb.

Weirdo.

After a diagnosis of dyslexia in her teens, Veda had worked hard on herself. Not only was she determined to walk back all the damage that came from hellish anxiety, lack of confidence, few friends and less hope, she had vowed to be stronger for it. And looking on the brighter side, finding ways to reclaim her self-esteem had laid the foundations for her career as a life coach, the most rewarding job on the planet. While she still battled nerves and always would, Veda could speak in front of an auditorium full of people now. She hadn't suffered one of her attacks where she strangled on her words in years.

Until now.

Ringing ears...closing throat...freezing brain.

"This has been weeks in the making," Hux said, looking around at the tented pavilion and its high-end fairy-tale trimmings. "Lanie and Susan's efforts, of course, not mine. Have you met Susan yet? She came down early to make sure everything was set."

As Hux waited for a reply, Veda's throat remained

squeezed shut. Cheeks flushed, she forced a smile and shook her head.

"Susan's a godsend," Hux went on. "Been with us for such a long time. She's phenomenal with the house and meals and, well, everything family."

Focused, trying to relax, Veda managed to squeak out, "I see."

Hux's smile dipped before he tried again. "When she arrived here, Susan knew nothing about horses or this kind of life. She loves the place now, of course, but she doesn't get much involved with that side of things."

Veda's mind was stuck. Words refused to come. And deep in her gut, tendrils of panic were spreading.

Lazy.

Dumb.

Weirdo.

Hux's eyes narrowed the barest amount before he tried a different approach. "I suppose you like horses, Veda? You've been around them most of your life."

"I... Horses are...beautiful."

He nodded like he hadn't worked her out yet and maybe didn't want to. "How's your dad doing?"

"Good. Busy." *Breathe, Veda. Just breathe.* "I'm staying there...this weekend."

"Right. The Darnel Stables aren't so far from here."

When she nodded again and took a sip from her champagne flute, Hux searched her eyes and then threw a look around. "Well, I'll let you get back to the party. Nice meeting you, Veda. Enjoy the night."

As he walked away, Veda let her smile and shoulders sag. Knowing next to no one here hadn't fazed her.

She could even deal with seeing Ajax again, however that turned out. But being left alone to talk with the man who years ago had let loose a storm of demons that had ultimately torn her family apart...

Veda didn't like to dwell on how much she'd cried when her parents had split, let alone the bombshell that had landed after that. But now, snapshots of events leading up to her mother's death broke through. And with the music getting louder and the crowd starting to press in—

She needed some space, some air, and she needed it now.

Setting her glass on a nearby table, Veda escaped through one of the pavilion's back exits, and she didn't stop going until she was cloaked in shadows and certain she was alone. Out here, the night air was so fresh and freeing. The beat of the music and drag of dark memories seemed just far enough away.

She was herding together more positive thoughts when, out of the shadows, a figure appeared. Dressed in a tuxedo now, Ajax was cutting the distance between them with a commanding gait. And the closer he got, the clearer the message grew in his gorgeous blue eyes.

You can run, sweetheart, it said, *but don't ever think you can hide.*

"If you want to leave, you're going the wrong way," Ajax said, tipping his head toward the house. "Cars are parked over there."

Taken aback, Veda blinked a few times before responding. "I wasn't leaving. I needed some air."

He forced a grin. "Like you needed air the night we met on that balcony a month ago."

Her knockout dress shimmered in the moonlight as she straightened. "Has it been that long?"

"Yup. That long."

After changing, Ajax had returned to the party pavilion in time to catch a flash of lipstick red as Veda dashed out the back. Of course, he had followed. He wanted to make sure she was all right. And, yes, he had also seen an opportunity to broach another sensitive matter. Namely, what the hell had happened after Saratoga? Why hadn't she accepted his calls?

Clearly, Veda wanted to avoid the subject.

"So, what are you doing out here in the dark?" she asked.

Ajax slid both hands into his pants pockets. "Psyching up for party mode?"

"Well, at least you're dressed for it now."

His smile was slow. "You saw me earlier?"

Her gorgeous green eyes widened before she visibly gathered herself again and offered a cool reply. "You got changed in record time."

"I'd already showered at the office." Grinning, he propped a shoulder against a nearby oak and crossed one ankle over the other. "I don't mind the smell of hay and horse, but I'm not sure the guests would appreciate it much."

When her gaze dipped to his mouth, he remembered back to that night and words she had murmured while nuzzling him from his chest all the way down.

You smell so good. And taste even better.

As if she was remembering, too, Veda threw a glance toward the lights and music. "I should get back."

"I'll walk with you." He pushed off the oak before adding, "If that's okay."

After a second's hesitation, she made a face like it was no big deal. "Sure," she said. "Why not."

As they headed back down a lit path, he set a leisurely pace. After the flowers and phone messages—after the multiple times she had come apart in his arms that wild night—had she even considered dropping him a line?

He studied her profile—straight nose, lush lips, laser-beam focus. And then there was that jaw-dropping dress. He couldn't help but imagine sliding the fabric from her shoulders, tracing the contours of her breasts with his lips…with his tongue…

Focus, damn it.

"Did you get my messages?" he asked after clearing his throat. "I left a couple."

"I did. The flowers, too. They were lovely."

Uh-huh.

"I wanted to let you know how much I enjoyed our time together."

Gaze still ahead, she nodded. "Thank you."

He nodded, too, scratched his ear. "We left Saratoga on pretty good terms, wouldn't you say?"

Her heels clicked a little faster on the path. "We should get back to the party."

"I thought we could talk."

"Maybe later."

He pulled up. *Maybe now.*

"Is this still about your dad, Veda? Because I thought we'd worked through that."

The train of her red gown swirled as she spun back around. "We agreed to disagree. Not the same thing."

Really? "That conversation happened right before we made love again. Before you said, 'I wish we never had to leave.'"

Her nostrils flared as she crossed her arms. "If you're trying to embarrass me, it won't work."

For the love of God. "I'm trying to understand why you didn't pick up the phone."

He didn't get how she could be all prickly one second and turned on to the hilt the next. Was she an ice queen or too hot to be believed?

She hesitated before taking two steps closer. "I'm guessing you didn't tell Lanie about that night."

What the—?

"Of course not. That's between you and me."

Cringing, she darted a look toward the party pavilion. "So put away the megaphone already."

He rubbed the back of his neck, lowered his voice. "I'm confused, okay? We don't need our parents' consent. We're not kids."

"Right. We're adults making up our own minds."

He groaned. "Still confused."

"I don't regret what happened between us that night. In fact, I'll remember it as long as I live."

So he hadn't imagined it. He wasn't going insane. But when he stepped closer, happy to get back on track, her hands shot up, stopping him dead.

"Ajax, you are wonderful in every conceivable way,"

she said. "I love spending time with you. The problem is... I'm not the only one. You're always in news feeds with models, actresses, designers, female ranch hands, trainers... There's been an endless string of women over the years. For God's sake, you're known as the Stud."

Ajax exhaled. First he'd had Lanie bleating in his ear. Now this?

Sure, his brothers had ribbed him about that *stud* label, a name some features reporter had come up with for a story a while back. But Griff and Jacob knew who he was.

"I'm a normal and, let me emphasize, *single* guy. Like you're a normal single woman. Dating is not a crime." His shoulders went back. "And there's nothing wrong with us wanting to see each other again."

"Wanting something doesn't necessarily make it good for you."

"Unless it is."

She tried another tack. "I don't approve of the business that you're in."

Say what now?

"You mean the stud farm? Which has stables for racehorses, which is the exact same business that your father is in."

"That doesn't mean *I* like it." She asked him, "Do you have any idea how many people lose their shirts at the track?"

"Veda, I can't help that."

"Like a dealer can't help an addict who continues to use?"

"Not the same thing."

"I'll fill you in on the definition of addiction some-day." She went on. "The worst part is the number of horses that are manipulated and hurt, too. Just last week, one of your own was put down after a fall."

He stiffened. "And let me tell you, I was upset about it."

"Not as upset as the horse."

He opened his mouth, stopped, and then sought clar-ification. "So you don't want to see me again because I own horses?"

"You *use* horses."

Whatever you want to call it. "That's not gonna change."

"No shit."

He had to grin. Veda could be direct when she wanted to be.

"Just please set me straight on one thing," he said. "You don't approve of keeping horses, but I don't hear you bawling out your bestie, the dressage champion."

"Lanie? That's…well, it's—"

"Please don't say *different*."

"Ajax, I'm not sleeping with your sister."

"Right." Stepping closer, he lowered his head over hers and ground out, "You're sleeping with me."

His whole body was a heartbeat as she gazed up with eyes flooding with questions. Veda might have her reasons for staying away, but he could tell a big part of her wanted Saratoga again at least as much as he did.

Finally she stepped back, took a breath.

"We're here for Lanie. This is her night."

He cast a look toward the twinkling pavilion and nodded. "Agreed."

"So we need to put this aside."

"That won't work."

"At least for now. For your sister's sake."

He slowly smiled. "You're a shrewd negotiator, Darnel."

"And you're a persistent SOB."

"One way to fix persistentness...because that's absolutely a word.".

She didn't hide her grin. "Okay."

"The point is, yes, we should rejoin the party, *and* have one drink together."

She cocked her head. "One drink?"

"Don't know about you, but I'm drier than a dust storm."

They continued down the path until Ajax had another thought and stopped again. "One more thing before we go in."

Veda sighed. "I'm going to regret this, aren't I?"

"I need to say how amazing you look tonight. That dress. Your hair." He slapped a hand over his heart. "And that's all I'll say on the subject. No more compliments."

And he meant it. Foot on the brake.

But one drink could always lead to two. Could maybe lead to...more.

Three

The woman who stopped beside Veda at the tent's buffet table came right out and said it.

"He's something else, isn't he?"

When the woman sent Ajax an approving look—he was talking with guests by the birthday cake—Veda's cheeks went warm. While looking over the desserts, every so often she had flickered a glance his way, obviously not as discreetly as she had thought.

And who was asking, anyway?

The woman was somewhere in her fifties and dressed in an elegant peach-colored sequined sheath. Her shoulder-length auburn hair was tucked behind an ear, revealing a dazzling teardrop diamond stud. Based on the woman's maternal smile as she continued to watch Ajax, Veda took a guess.

"You're Susan, aren't you? Hux Rawson's…house-keeper."

After many years, it was known among relevant circles that the pair was less employee and boss these days and more a couple without the legal formalities.

Susan's dimpled smile grew. "I met Ajax when he was a teen. Now he's like my own. The other kids, too."

After Veda introduced herself—leaving out her last name, which might complicate things at this time of night—Susan looked Ajax's way again. As she leaned back against a column, her expression deepened. "Did you know that boy is the reason I'm here?"

"Really? How's that?"

The lights dimmed at the same time Veda settled in for what promised to be an interesting conversation.

"After their mom passed away," Susan explained, "the family was devastated, as you can imagine. With his father so lost in his grief, Ajax decided to step up to the plate. He placed an advertisement in the local paper. *We need a housekeeper*, the ad read. *Someone who would like a family to look after. On my word, we will look after you right back.*"

Veda's heart squeezed. "That is so sweet."

"I'd been going through some difficulties myself. Not a death, thank heaven. But enough to spin my world around 'til I didn't know which way was up. Life can be like that sometimes. Downright dizzying." Straightening, she resurrected her gentle smile. "I got the job and haven't looked back since. I've never felt more fulfilled. I'd always wanted children of my own, so those kids were the icing on my cake. Griff, Ajax, Lanie and, of course, Jacob."

Lanie had mentioned Griff, the Wall Street kingpin, as well as her adopted brother, whom she idolized as much as the other two. "Jacob's a lawyer, right?"

"With an outstanding reputation. He came to us through a juvie program." She toyed with the diamond stud as she clarified, "For years, Huxley ran a scheme here for boys in trouble who might benefit from fresh scenery and a little guidance. While they helped with chores, they learned about responsibility as well as what they were capable of and, more importantly, what they deserved out of life. Jacob had a terrible childhood, but Huxley saw something very special in that boy. He decided to fill the void and give him a real home."

Veda's chest tightened and expanded all at once. It was easy to tell that Susan had a generous heart, like Veda's mom, who had always been willing to see the best in people. Sometimes that kind of faith was uplifting. At other times, it was naive. Even foolish.

As the music segued into a slower, older tune, Susan glanced up at speakers hidden among the fairy lights. "Oh, I love this song."

The lyrics spoke of stars falling from the sky and longing to be close to someone.

Veda smiled. "I know it."

"I was so young when it came out. Back then I couldn't imagine having a gray hair or wrinkle. Time's so precious. The most precious thing we have." She held Veda's gaze when she emphasized, "Once it's gone, there's no getting it back."

Just then, Veda felt Ajax glance her way. While his gaze, curious and hot, locked with hers through the crowd, Susan straightened.

"Well, I'm going to find someone to share this dance with." As she headed off, Susan gave Veda a wink. "Maybe you should, too."

Perhaps it was the commanding picture Ajax painted in that crisp tuxedo, the knowing smile hovering at the corners of his mouth, or simply the song that amplified the moment. For whatever reason, when Ajax looked between her and the dance floor and then raised his brows in suggestion, Veda felt slightly light-headed. A little too eager to agree.

Since sharing that drink earlier, the anticipation had only built…delicious, taut and unrelenting. Now, as Ajax extended his arms in the air in front of him like he was already slow-dancing with her, Veda felt an unraveling. Like a corset being unlaced. Like she could finally breathe out and relax.

Time *was* precious, and this night and its challenges were almost over. Wasn't this an appropriate and mature way to say goodbye?

She walked toward him. He met her halfway. After taking her hand in his much larger, far warmer one, he turned to escort her to the dance floor. Once they were surrounded by other couples, Ajax positioned their joined hands higher near his lapel while his free palm slid around to rest against the sensitive small of her back. As he smiled into her eyes, she quivered with the same kind of longing the song spoke about. Which was only to be expected, and nothing she couldn't handle. And when they began to move, his expert steps guiding hers, she was okay with his strength and his touch. She had no trouble owning her body's response to his scent and his heat.

"You met Susan," he said.

"She's a big fan of yours."

"Ah, she likes everyone. Heart of gold."

"She said you're the reason she's here."

His smile kicked up one corner of his mouth again. "The first time we met, I knew she'd fit in. Turns out, even better than I hoped. She and Dad have more than a professional relationship now. They're more than friends."

"But they never married."

While he thought that through, his hot palm shifted on her back—moving slightly lower, pressing harder. "I've never asked why. Not my business. They're happy. That's what it's all about."

As his gaze brushed her cheek, then her lips, the sexual pull tugged even more strongly. Everything about him was soothing, beguiling, on top of being sexy to a giddy fault. If he ever took a page from his father's book and settled down, all Veda could say was that his wife would be a very lucky girl.

Lanie was dancing nearby, but she didn't seem to notice them, or anyone else for that matter. Rather she looked besotted with her partner, a classic tall, dark and incredibly handsome type. Interesting. Lanie was supposed to be into her career way more than the opposite sex. It was one of the things the two women had bonded over.

Veda asked Ajax, "Who's Lanie dancing with?"

Ajax didn't turn around to check. Instead the two couples drifted farther apart.

"Lanie has a lot of friends."

Veda nodded at the crowd. "At least a couple hundred."

"You wouldn't know it now, but once upon a time she was shy. Guess we all outgrow that childhood stuff."

Veda recalled Susan's story about the kid who had taken over the reins in an effort to help his grieving family. She couldn't imagine Ajax ever being awkward, lacking confidence, doubting himself or not having just the right words. Having just the right *everything*.

The song finished up. As the DJ cued his upcoming selection, the moment stretched out. Veda and Ajax looked into each other's eyes and invisible strings worked to tug them even closer together. When the DJ played a faster, louder song, Ajax led her through the crowd to a quieter semi-hidden corner where blinking lights didn't quite penetrate and only the most curious eyes might see. As they faced each other again, with his hand still holding hers, the physical awareness zapping between them became fully charged. She imagined what might come next…

Would Ajax lift her chin and claim his first kiss of the evening?

If she let that happen, she'd be lost.

Sucking down a breath, Veda shored herself up and announced, "I'm going to call it a night."

His head went back. "You mean *now*?"

"It's getting late." They had less than an hour until midnight. "No one's left that I know."

"You know *me*."

Intimately. But better to avoid that fact.

"Lanie's obviously occupied for a while." Veda remembered how entranced her friend had looked with her dance partner. She wouldn't interrupt that chemistry to say good-night. "I'll call and check in with her tomorrow."

"You're not staying over? I thought Lanie might have offered you a—"

"I'm staying at Dad's tonight."

A couple of days ago, she had called to give her father a heads-up. When she'd dropped in there earlier today to stash her overnight bag and change, he had been reading a book in his favorite chair. He had complimented her gown, adding, "It must be a swanky event." When Veda admitted that she was going to help celebrate Lanie's birthday at the Rawson property, her father's fingers had tightened around the book. He had restrained himself from trying to talk her out of entering enemy territory, although he had made it clear that he would be waiting up.

Now, from their tucked-away vantage point, Ajax studied the scene again. The party had changed gears, entering the phase when formalities were over. Plenty of guests were still here, happy to let loose. Plenty of women with whom Ajax could become well acquainted.

But he only tugged at his bow tie and released a couple of shirt buttons as he said, "I should call it a night, too. Big day tomorrow. I'll walk you to your car."

It had rained earlier. Crossing from the shelter of the tent onto a wet path, Veda scooped up as much of her mermaid dress train as she could. After a few steps, however, some of it slipped, dropping right into a puddle. She was about to dive and rescue what she could, but Ajax had already gone into action.

As if she weighed no more than a bagful of petals, he scooped her up into his arms. When Veda flipped the fabric up and over her lap, Ajax's gaze caught hers.

"All good?" he asked.

She almost sighed. "All good."

As they left the party noise behind, rather than focus on her body's reaction to being pressed up against so much Rawson muscle and heat, she did her best to concentrate on something else.

"When was the family house built?" she asked, studying the majestic shingle-style Victorian.

"The original place was built a hundred and forty years ago," he said, his big shoulders rolling as she gently rocked to the swing of his step. "It's still standing just a little north of here."

Veda wondered if it was anything like the original Darnel house, a gorgeous but pint-size stone structure that she used whenever she stayed over now.

"This house," Ajax went on, "was built around ten

years later. It's been extended and modernized, but its heart is the same. Earthy. Solid."

Through some living room windows, she saw a wall filled with family portraits—some recent, others obviously going back years. There wasn't a single photo displayed in her father's house anywhere—not of family or graduation. Certainly not of a wedding.

As those portraits slid out of view, Veda sighed. "Lots of happy memories."

"Oh, man, I had the *best* childhood. This was a great place to grow up, and with fantastic parents." As they passed beneath an overhead light, Veda watched a pulse begin to beat in his jaw as his grin faded. "Things changed after Mom died, of course. But we got through it. In some ways, we're even stronger."

Veda was happy for them. Was even envious, as a matter of fact. What she wouldn't give to have been part of a big, happy family. How different her life would have been.

"I didn't get to meet Griff or Jacob tonight," she said, "but they looked proud standing behind Lanie with you all before the cake was cut." After a brief speech, she had thanked everyone for coming; some guests were from as far away as Argentina, Australia and the Netherlands. Lanie's dressage events took her all over the world.

"Yeah. Great night. And tomorrow morning, over a huge breakfast, all the highlights will be rehashed and new stories shared…until we're all asking about lunch."

When he chuckled, Veda noticed that her hand had come to rest upon his chest. Along with the gravelly vibration, she could actually feel his heartbeat against her palm. Then he looked down into her eyes and everything else receded into the background at the same time his gorgeous grin seemed to gravitate a smidgeon closer.

If I wound my fingers into his lapel... she thought, *...if I edged up a little and he edged down...*

Then—thank God—they arrived at her SUV. Ajax lowered her onto her feet and, as Veda admired his profile—the high brow, hawkish nose and shadowed granite jaw—he gave a thumbs-up to the ad panel for her business painted on the door.

"Best Life Now," he said. "I like it. Real catchy." He nodded like he was invested. Like he sincerely wanted to know more. "So how does a person do that—have their best life now? Do you give talks? Teach classes?"

"I do both." She delivered her automatic line for anyone who showed interest. "You ought to come along to a self-improvement seminar sometime."

Not that she could possibly tutor him on anything in that regard. Ajax had his life all sorted out. He was exactly where, and how, he wanted to be.

He crossed his arms and assumed a stance that said she had his full attention. "Give me the elevator pitch."

"You can achieve your best life now by behaving your way to happiness and success," she replied. "Start with healthy habits and surround yourself with the best. The best friends, the best information, the best advice, *and* be smart enough to take it. You should also go after the things that matter to you the most. Everyone needs to get behind themselves and push."

"Sure." He shrugged. "Get up in the morning and get things done."

Spoken like someone who'd always had his shit together.

"Did you know that some people struggle to even roll out of bed in the morning? And you need to look beyond the rationale of just being lazy."

"Look beyond it to what?"

"Maybe past trauma, dysfunctional family, learned helplessness."

His eyebrows drew together. "You can learn to be helpless?"

"Sure. It can happen if a person feels like they can't stop the bad stuff from happening, so they just give up."

The same way Veda had wanted to give up after her mom had died. She wasn't able to save the person she had loved most in the world. Worse, she had felt responsible for the accident. Constant feelings of worthlessness coupled with guilt had added up to a *why the hell bother?* mind-set.

Ajax's expression changed as his eyes searched hers. "There's a whole lot more to you, isn't there, Darnel?"

"A few layers. Like most people."

The perfect Ajax comeback line might be, *And I want to peel back every one, starting here, tonight.* But there were parts of Veda no one would ever know. Not her father or Lanie. Not Veda's Best Life Now clients or blog followers. And certainly not Ajax Rawson... family rival, player extraordinaire and proponent of an industry that she wished would disappear.

As if he'd read her mind, Ajax's jaw tightened and

his chin kicked up. Then, rather than delivering a line, he did something that pulled the rug right out from under her feet. He took a measured step back, slipped both hands under his jacket and into his pants pockets. The body language was clear.

Nothing more to say. Won't hold you up.

After a recalibrating moment, Veda got her rubbery mouth to work. "Well, Ajax…it was good to see you again."

"You, too, Veda. Take care. Stay well."

When he didn't offer a platonic kiss on her cheek—when he only pushed his hands deeper into his pockets—she gave a definitive nod before climbing into her car. But she hadn't started the engine before his face appeared inches away from her window.

The nerves in Veda's stomach knotted even tighter. Damn, she had to give it to this man. He'd waited until the very last minute, wanting to catch her completely off guard to ask if he could see her again.

Channeling *aloof*, Veda pressed a button. As the window whirred down, she got ready for an extra-smooth delivery. But Ajax only pointed down the driveway.

"Take it slow down the hill," he said. "There's a sharp bend near the office."

She blinked. "A bend?"

"It'll be wet after the rain."

When he stepped back again, Veda took a moment before winding the window back up, starting the car and driving away.

So…

Score, right?

Rather than trying to charm or argue with her, Ajax had given her what she wanted. A cut-and-dried goodbye. And the bonus: she wasn't the one receding in Ajax's rearview mirror. *He* was receding in *hers*. In fact, watching his reflection now, she saw how he was literally walking away.

Sighing, Veda settled in for the drive home—or tried to. After being so close to Ajax and his drugging scent, the car smelled stale, and following hours of music and conversation, the cabin was too quiet. Veda flicked on the radio, but she only heard that song playing in her head...the one she and Ajax had danced to all of ten minutes ago.

She shook herself. Thought ahead.

In thirty minutes, she would be turning into the Darnel driveway. She would find her father reclined in his tufted high-backed chair by an unlit fire. After inquiring about her evening, he would calmly regurgitate how he felt about his daughter consorting with the enemy. The Rawsons were cheats who would have their comeuppance. Drake never tired of admitting that he couldn't wait for the day.

Veda sat forward and looked up. Raindrops were falling again, big and hard on the windshield. She switched on the wipers, imagining her father's reaction should he ever discover the truth. Not only was his daughter friends with a Rawson, she had also—shock, horror!—slept with one. In his chilling way, Drake would let her know his verdict. She was no better than the woman he had loved *or* the woman he had married. To his mind, both had betrayed him with a cowboy.

Then her father would disown his daughter, the same way he had disowned his wife. And there wouldn't be a thing she could do about it.

You are dead to me.

Dead. Dead. Dead.

Suddenly that tricky bend was right there in front of her. About to overshoot, Veda wrenched the wheel, slammed on the brake. As her tires slid out, she pulled the wheel the other way and the SUV overcorrected. A surreal moment later, it came to a jolting stop on the grass shoulder, at right angles to a heavy railed fence and the sweeping river of asphalt.

With those wipers beating endlessly back and forth, Veda white-knuckled the wheel, cursing her inattention. Her stupidity. But thankfully, she hadn't crashed. There was nothing that couldn't be undone. *So pull up your big-girl panties and get back on the road!* And she would…as soon as she'd dealt with the tsunami of déjà vu rolling in.

Mom sitting in the front seat of a growling pickup truck. Her cowboy boyfriend looking over his shoulder at Veda in back. A terrifying screech. A crashing, blinding jolt—

When her ears started to ring, Veda pushed open her door and scrambled out.

There were plenty of motels around. Or maybe she should simply drive on through to Jersey. She was under no obligation to see her father tonight. Damn it, her only obligation was to herself.

Not my fault, not my fault, not my fault.

At that moment, just as the skies opened up in earnest, a pair of big hands clamped down on her shoulders and spun her around. With hair whipping over her eyes, it took a moment to recognize the masculine figure, and then the concerned face streaming with rain.

Ajax raised his voice over the downpour. "What the hell are you doing?"

Veda thought about it and shrugged. "I don't know."

His brows snapped together before he threw open the back car door and waved an arm.

Get in.

The next second, he was behind the wheel, getting the vehicle back onto the driveway before turning, not toward the house or the main road, but into an offshoot lane. A moment later, they'd pulled up outside a building. After helping Veda out, he handed over her evening clutch from the front passenger seat and led the way to the building's main entrance.

Soaked through, her soles sliding in their heels, she asked over the noise of the rain, "Where are we?"

"Somewhere safe."

And yet, as Ajax punched numbers into a control pad by the door, the sign mounted next to it seemed to both mock and warn her.

Rawson Studs.

Satisfaction guaranteed.

Four

Entering the office reception area and flicking on the lights, Ajax was torn between a slump of relief and thinking, what the hell?

So much for carrying Veda over those puddles earlier. Now her hair and dress were drenched. Worse—and no surprise—she was visibly shaken. He could practically hear her teeth chattering. Had she been playing with her phone or simply off with the fairies when she'd overrun that bend? The bend he'd specifically told her to watch out for.

With Veda close behind, he strode down the corridor, past some other offices and into his private office suite—his home away from home. Running a hand through his dripping hair, he took it down a notch. And then two. The last thing she needed was a grilling. Far better that he shake it off.

"I vote scotch," he said, making a beeline for the wet bar and pouring two stiff ones. But when he brought hers over, Veda's nostrils flared like he was offering week-old hog feed.

"I don't drink hard liquor," she said.

"Fine." He lifted the glass and tossed it back. "Bottoms up."

After the heat hit his gut, Ajax found the bar again. "I'll get you a wine."

"Just water," she said. "Although… I've probably had enough of that for one night."

Enough water? Because of the rain and almost killing herself? But he didn't laugh.

Despite dancing together and their too-hot-to-ignore connection, by the time he'd escorted—no, literally carried—her to her vehicle, he'd made a decision. If Veda really wanted him to take a hike, he would comply, at least for now. So he had played nice and said good-night. Thank God he turned back around when he did. Seeing her almost take out that fence had scared the living daylights out of him. Veda must have gotten the fright of her life.

But now as she accepted the tumbler of water, he noticed her hands had stopped shaking. After taking a long sip, she let her head rock back and eased out a breath.

"I'm sorry, Ajax," she said, looking so vulnerable and bedraggled and all the more beautiful because of it.

With the tightness easing in his chest, he hitched up

a shoulder and swirled his drink. "Ah, you're not hurt. That's what matters."

"I'll get out of your hair as soon as the rain stops. Promise. I don't want to hold you up."

Veda wasn't an inconvenience. He wished she'd just relax. That was sure as hell what he intended to do.

She pushed aside the wet hair clinging to her cheek and neck. "Do you mind if I take my shoes off?"

"Be my guest."

While she sat down on the couch to slip off her heels, Ajax shed his jacket and plucked at his soaked shirt.

"I need to change." He considered her soggy dress. "I can offer you a towel and a clean shirt."

Getting to her bare feet, she held up the waterlogged hem of her dress. "I'll take it."

Ajax slipped into the attached private suite where he spent most nights, and grabbed a freshly pressed shirt from the walk-in closet next to the bed. Back in the main area, he held the button-down out to Veda.

"How's this?"

"It's dry—so, perfect."

He pointed her to a guest bathroom with plenty of towels. As soon as she disappeared behind the door, he headed for his room again, ripping his shirt off as he went. After ditching everything else in a corner— shoes, socks, pants—he towel-dried his hair in the attached bathroom, then found a pair of drawstring pants. That's when his phone sounded in the next room. He recognized the ringtone.

Griff.

Hopping as he slotted each leg into the pants, he recovered the phone from his jacket's inside pocket.

"Your lights are on," Griff said when Ajax connected. "Want company? I have some stuff to unpack."

Glancing toward the guest bathroom, Ajax lowered his voice. "What's wrong?"

"Not so much outright wrong as possibly troubling."

"To do with family or business?"

"Both. I'll come down and we'll hash it out."

Ajax grasped for an excuse. "It's raining."

Silence on the other end of the line ended with a grunt.

"Okay. Got it. You have someone squirreled away with you down there."

Ajax was shaking his head. "Not what you think."

"Bro, you don't need to play Boy Scout with me."

"She had a little accident going down."

Griff cleared his throat. "Okay. Not touching that one."

"Going down the entrance road. Her car skidded out."

Griff's tone changed. "Is she all right?"

"Shaken, but otherwise fine."

"I'd ask if there was anything I can do but I'm sure you've got it in hand. Or she has."

He and Griff were of a similar mind where the opposite sex was concerned. Unlike their brother Jacob, who had recently found the girl of his dreams, neither Ajax nor Griff was ready to settle down. They dated freely and widely and, more often than not, were with women who shared the same philosophy.

Given what Lanie had said earlier, and Veda's comments about men with reputations, his current guest did not subscribe to that particular point of view, which didn't gel with her enthusiasm in Saratoga, but whatever.

Absently pulling the string on his pants tighter, Ajax said again, "Griff, this is not a hookup."

"So you two definitely won't end up naked together tonight."

Ajax looked down at his bare chest at the same time he imagined Veda's dress puddled on that bathroom floor as Griff went on. "Look, we'll catch up over breakfast. You ought to bring her along."

"Why would I do that?"

"Gee, I don't know. Manners? Food?"

"Veda won't be here in the morning."

Even if he and Veda *did* spend the night together—say, she curled up on a couch, shut her eyes and fell dead asleep—neither would want that kind of morning-after scrutiny. Yes, they were adults who were more than capable of making adult decisions. But after that "eyes and hands off" talk, Princess Lanie would blow a gasket if he walked into the house with her bestie hanging off his arm. And Veda had that thing going on in her head about Hux—the story where he was supposed to have stolen Drake's future bride. *As if.*

"Wait a minute," Griff said. "Did you say Veda? As in Darnel's daughter?"

Ajax groaned. "Don't tell me you've got problems with that, too?"

"I, uh…" Griff exhaled. "Jax, we'll talk in the morning, okay?"

Ajax was signing off when the guest bathroom door fanned open. As Veda stepped out, every cell in his body stood to attention. The button-down shirt she wore was ten sizes too big, her towel-dried hair was a flaming mess, and what he could see of her legs made his mouth water. The unconscious way she used both hands to push back all that hair told him she felt more relaxed. Then she stopped, her eyes grew to saucers, and Ajax remembered.

She was the only one wearing a shirt.

He'd swear on the Bible that was not intentional.

"I, uh, got caught up on a call," he said, waving the phone.

Veda's gaze slid up from his chest.

"It was Griff," he said. "My brother. He saw the lights on here, so I filled him in."

"As in, I'm an idiot?"

"As in we need reflector lights on that curve."

When her eyes dipped to his chest again, Ajax re-evaluated his position. He definitely had *not* brought Veda here to seduce her. Before his phone had rung, he'd had every intention of slipping on a T-shirt. But now he got the distinct impression that Veda wasn't about to freak at his lack of clothing. Hell, she'd seen him in way less than this.

Veda was crossing over to his desk. He'd left his hat by a stack of papers. Now she ran a finger around the black brim, then sent a bland glance his way.

"Every cowboy needs one."

"At *least* one. That particular hat's for dressing up." Like for meetings, events. He nodded at another Stetson on a vintage hat stand. "That one's for work." For when he was hands-on in the stables with the horses and his team.

She picked up the formal hat and sussed out its lines as he wandered over.

"I reckon it'd suit you," he said.

"Pretty sure you're wrong."

He took the hat, but when he placed it on her head, the brim fell low enough to cover her nose. He saw her grin before repositioning the inner band so that it was propped against the front of her crown.

"There now," he said. "Not too big at all."

"All I need is a set of spurs and a big ol' buckle on my belt—"

The hat slipped again. As she caught it and pushed it back up, he angled her around toward some mirrored wall tiles. Setting her hands on her hips, she struck an Annie Oakley pose, then pulled a face.

"Yeah, nah." She lifted the hat off her head as she turned back around. "Bend down."

She set the Stetson square on his head, then stepped back to inspect her work. As she took him in from top to tail, her grin changed from light and playful to *we're having too much fun here*.

Putting her weight on one leg, she crossed her arms. "Your other hat's black, too."

"Yep. All of them from day one."

"Which was…?"

"When did I get my first real cowboy hat?" He

scratched his temple under the brim. "I can't remember ever being without one." When her lips twitched, like he'd said something funny, he frowned. "What's the joke?"

"It's just…at the risk of inflating your ego, you look like you ought to be on a billboard right now."

He flicked a glance up at the brim. "You like the hat that much?"

"I like the overall picture. Who wouldn't?" She seemed to gather herself, adjusting the oversize shirt's collar, before assuming an indifferent expression. "Just an observation."

Ajax's smile grew. "An observation, huh?"

"The hat, the smile. You know…" She fluttered her hands at his chest.

Chewing his inner lip, Ajax grinned more.

"I think you're flirting with me," he said.

She rolled her eyes. "I am not."

"You definitely are, and you know it."

"Ajax, I've never said you weren't sexy."

"Double negative, but go on."

"That's it." She glanced at his chest *again*, then, just as fast, looked away. "You can stop fishing for compliments."

"Well, I have something to say."

"Of course you do."

"You seem okay now. After that incident in your car."

"I am. Thanks again."

"And one other thing."

"Let me guess. You think I'm sexy, too."

Well, yeah. But that aside…

"Just thought you'd like to know—" he nodded toward the window "—the rain stopped five minutes ago."

Ohmigod!

He was doing it again. Being all mind-bendingly gorgeous, having her believe he was about to make a big move, and then—

And then—

Veda spun toward the window.

The rain had stopped?

"I thought it was still pouring."

"Nope." He rubbed his knuckles over his shadowed jaw as he peered out the window, too. "Guess it could start again, though."

Before she thought to stop herself, Veda smiled. "Yes, it could."

"But you said you wanted to leave as soon as it eased off. So, to be safe, you should probably make a break for it now."

That teasing grin, the mischievous glint in his dreamy blue eyes... He was just so full of it.

"You love playing with me, don't you?"

His smoldering grin spread wider. "I'll go with yes."

She'd put it another way. "You don't really want me to go."

"Wait. *You* were the one who said you wanted to leave. I'm merely respecting your wishes. Keeping you up to date. Making sure any possibility of you and me getting together again tonight is categorically off the table." He shrugged his broncobusting shoulders. "That *is* what you want, right?"

While his chin tilted downward so that the brim of his hat almost covered the gleam in his eyes, Veda froze. What was the right response? She wasn't completely sure anymore. The spinout in her car had brought back some ugly memories. Now she was with the man who had stormed down that hill in the rain to rescue her, which had made her feel not just good but safe.

And yet Ajax was the furthest thing from that. He was a prince in the art of seduction. He was in love with an industry she loathed.

For God's sake, he was a Rawson.

"I can see you're frustrated," he went on.

She grunted and shifted on her feet. "A little."

"Would you like me to fix that for you?"

Like how? By kissing her senseless?

He was blindly laying the hat on the desk while he studied her face and hair like she was a fine piece of art. Like he could devour her whole in one big-bad-wolf bite.

"Veda? You okay?"

She held her nervy stomach. "I'm not sure."

His gaze raked over her again, drawing out the moment, leaving her to wince and wonder and wait.

"You know," he finally said, "I wasn't going to push it, but we need to do this. We need to quit playing games."

"Playing games?"

"Come on, Veda. You know what I'm talking about. Just be honest and say it—"

"Okay, okay! We do. We need to talk."

A muscle in his jaw jumped before he gave a slow,

approving nod. "So you agree. We need to be open about how we feel."

"And then what?"

"Then we need to do something about it."

"You mean the same something we did in Saratoga."

He moved closer, until his breath warmed her brow and the energy arcing from his body to hers could be measured in megawatts.

In his lowest, sexiest voice, he said, "I'm going to kiss you now."

Her insides began to throb. To beg. "Why…why are you telling me that?"

"I want to know you're okay with it."

"You didn't ask the first time you kissed me."

"Did you want me to?"

"No."

"And now?"

She blinked, then gave it up. "I suppose you can tell me what to expect."

His lidded gaze dropped and locked on her mouth. "This kiss will be soft and light. Just a taste. Just in case. Then, if you're absolutely sure, I'll kiss you again. Deeper and longer next time."

She croaked, "And then…?"

"Then…" He studied her shirt. "That'll need to go."

She swallowed and pushed out a quivery breath.

"Ajax…?"

"Yes, Veda?"

"I'm not wearing anything underneath."

His grin grew. "I was hoping you'd say that."

Five

This time four weeks ago, she and Ajax had been in Saratoga Springs. As they strolled around a garden after the charity event, there hadn't been a cloud in the jasmine-scented moonlit sky. She remembered how he had stopped to cup her face and then kiss her like no woman had ever been kissed before. In that instant, it was all over.

She was his.

For years, she had dreamed of Ajax Rawson telling her she was beautiful, making her blush. But that night he'd done so much more than that. He had lifted her up. Helped her to fly.

After parting ways, she'd decided that had to be a one-time-only experience. And yet, as his lips met hers now and sparks began to ignite, Veda only wanted to know that kind of ecstasy again. Suddenly all she cared about was Ajax, all night long.

That didn't change when his mouth claimed hers and she found out he had lied. This wasn't soft and light, or just a taste just in case. This was as deliberate as any kiss got. And then his arms wound around her, urging her in, and her hands found his chest, hard and hot just as she remembered. When her fingertips grazed his nipples, she felt his grin before he deepened the kiss…so penetrating and skilled, her blood felt on fire.

While she reacquainted herself with his shoulders and pecs, his hands trailed down her back until they were under her shirttails, kneading her buns. After each loving squeeze, his fingers slid together, scooping between the backs of her thighs. When Veda lifted a knee against the outside of his leg, his tongue stopped stroking hers for a beat before his touch went deeper, sliding along her sex. Each time he dipped a finger inside, pressing on just the right spot, she inched that knee a little higher and held on that bit tighter.

"I've thought about you every day," he murmured against her lips.

"Me, too," she sighed. "I've thought of you."

His jaw grazed her cheek. "Next time, you'll answer my calls."

She couldn't stop grinning. "Just try to get me off the phone."

He hooked both hands between the backs of her thighs, coaxing her legs apart as he effortlessly raised her up. As her feet left the floor and her legs looped around him, she clung to his neck before his mouth took hers again. Cradling her seat, he rotated her hips, pressing her closer, stoking that heat.

And as his hold grew firmer and the grinding got more intense, the friction began to climb…dear Lord, it began to blaze.

That night in Saratoga, Veda had given herself to him completely despite being nervous as hell. Ajax remembered how she had blushed while he'd gotten her out of that dress…how she had hesitated that first time climbing on top. Being with Veda had felt different.

Had felt…new.

Tonight, however, the training wheels were off. In no time, they had gone from kissing to full steam ahead. Now her legs were lashed around his hips, and every time he pushed in against her, the bulge in his pants just grew and grew.

Breaking the kiss, he set his chin on her forehead, found his breath and drilled down on necessities.

"Protection," he said.

Her teeth grazed his Adam's apple. "We need that."

As he resumed their kiss, her hand dipped under his waistband and coiled around his erection. It felt good. *Very* good. Dropping her weight a little, he balanced her on his thighs to give her a little more room.

A moment later, he fought through the pheromone fog to ask and be sure. "You're on the pill, though, right?"

Her grip on his neck slipped. At the same time he caught her, he moved to brace a palm against the nearest wall. A heartbeat later, she eased up and positioned the tip of his shaft precisely where it needed to be.

After that initial bolt of pleasure, he began to move. Not in careful, gentle *we'll get there* pumps. Tonight she obviously didn't need slow and steady, and you'd better believe, neither did he.

Her fingers were in his hair, knotting through the back, plowing up the sides, and he was wishing it hadn't been so long between encounters because nothing felt like this… Veda here with him now and all brakes off, letting him know that her reasons for staying away didn't matter anymore.

Or at least didn't matter tonight.

As her legs vised tighter and his hold on her butt grew firmer, perspiration broke out on his brow, down his back. And then the responsible side of his brain kicked in again. *No glove, bro, no love.* Being inside her again was better than anything. But he needed to rein it in. For a start, he wanted to satisfy her first.

But it seemed, on that score, she was way ahead of him.

He was about to pull out when she ground in that much harder, deeper, at the same time her legs locked around him extra tight. When her head arced back, she shuddered and convulsed as her mouth dropped open and her nails bit into his neck.

God! There was so much steam and energy. Such intensity and blinding, shooting heat.

That was the second Ajax realized he'd just crossed the finish line, too.

Six

Amazing wasn't the right word. It wasn't nearly big or, well, *real* enough. With early-morning light filtering in through the windows, and Veda still asleep, the best Ajax could come up with to describe last night's reunion was explosive.

Lying beside her, facing her, he played with a wave of her hair as he recalled the conflagration when they'd come together. He'd been acutely aware of the heat as it built, the speed with which it had grown. But that tandem climax had caught him completely off guard.

Afterward, Ajax had carried her in here to the bedroom where they'd scrapped her shirt and his pants and played around in a warm sudsy shower. There'd been plenty of exaggerated lathering and just as much kissing. But after toweling off, they'd slipped under these sheets, snuggled up and fallen asleep.

As he'd drifted off, Ajax had embraced the feeling. Absolutely, without question, he'd been satisfied like never before. Now he wanted to coax her awake and not only recapture it all, but go harder and deeper.

He wanted to know so much more.

Veda stirred. Tangles of red hair glistened in the muted light as she stretched and sighed and eventually blinked open her eyes. She smelled of soap, remnants of her citrusy perfume and a natural scent that aroused him possibly even more than the sight of her breasts peeking above the rumpled sheet. He wanted to trace the tip of his tongue around each nipple, nip and gently suck the tips.

Instead he brushed his lips over hers. When she sighed again, sleepily smiling into his eyes, he ran a palm up her side. As he found her breast, she slid her fingers back through his hair.

Angling his head, he kissed her slowly and emphatically while he rolled her nipple between a finger and thumb. Then, moving closer, he pressed in against her belly, letting her know how darn turned on he was. He loved making her come, making her happy. He couldn't think of a better way to kick off a lazy Sunday morning. Hell, if it was up to him, he'd spend the whole day here. The whole week.

Then Veda paused and shifted onto her back. Maybe she wanted him to use his mouth instead. He was only too happy to oblige.

But as he moved to go down, she caught his shoulder. Her voice was croaky but firm.

"What time is it?"

Ajax leaned in to circle the tip of his nose around hers. "Doesn't matter."

"It *so* matters."

A few moments earlier, he'd caught the time on his wristwatch on the bedside table. "A little after seven."

She shut her eyes and groaned. "I need to go."

"You do not need to go." He knew where she was headed with this, but right now they needed the outside world to butt out. "If you're worried about what anyone might think—" like Lanie or Hux, or Griff, who'd called it last night on the phone "—this is none of their business."

"It would just be so much easier—"

"You know what would be easier?" he cut in, edging closer. "If we finished what we're doing now. And later, you come up to the house and have breakfast."

She blinked like he was talking Mandarin. And, yes, he'd baulked at that breakfast idea, too, when Griff had suggested it. But now, after being with Veda again, extending that invitation seemed like the obvious thing to do. He didn't want to shoo Veda off like he was ashamed or some kind of prick.

"Sorry," she said, pushing up onto an elbow. "I don't work that way. I'm not going to flaunt it."

Ah, hell. He'd come right out and say it then. "You mean because your father wouldn't approve?"

Her eyes widened. "My father wouldn't be the only one knocked off his chair." She stopped, seemed to remember something and then cursed under her breath. "I forgot to call to say not to wait up."

"Your father was waiting up for you?" Really? How old was she again?

"It's his house. I am his daughter."

"And you're over twenty-one."

She switched tacks. "What about Lanie? What's she going to think?"

When she found out that her friend and brother had spent the night together? "Lanie wouldn't expect this. But she'll support you because that's what friends do. Siblings, too, for that matter."

He pushed up to sit against the headboard. Veda took her time but finally joined him. Wrapping his arm around her, he nuzzled her sweet-smelling hair and waited. He'd said enough. Time for her speak.

Bit by bit, he felt her relax. Eventually, she laid a palm on his chest.

"When I drove away last night," she said, "I was… distracted. Thinking about Dad and how he would react if he knew…"

Drake might get his nose out of joint, but dude. Suck it up. Except Veda didn't need to hear that.

Ajax stroked her arm, nuzzled her again.

"I'm sorry," he said.

"Sorry we got together, or sorry that my father's against anything Rawson?"

"Veda, I don't care what Drake thinks about me or my family. I care about how you feel."

She paused before she rubbed her cheek against his shoulder, nodding.

"I want to tell you something else," she said.

He held her a little tighter. "Shoot."

"When we were younger, I had a massive crush on you. I'd go to a race with my father and see you there with your dad. You were this tall, blond, muscle-ripped dream. Always smiling and talking. But I think an even bigger part of the attraction was knowing you were taboo. Forbidden. And even though I've moved away and have my own place and my own views, I always felt that was a place I could never go."

Ajax's gut was in knots. Imagine growing up in the cold shadow of a father like Drake Darnel. Sure, Ajax liked having his own father's approval, particularly when it came to looking after the farm and the business. Hux's middle name was High Standards. But they were still their own people who enjoyed a mutual respect. There was trust. A certain understanding.

Which was obviously not the case where Veda and Drake were concerned.

"So don't tell your father," he said. The silly old coot didn't need to know.

"It's too late for that. My car is parked right out front. Whether or not I sit down for breakfast with your family, rumors will spread. They always do."

"My family isn't into gossip, Veda."

"Maybe not. But you have how many employees? Riders, assistant trainers, grooms, barn and breeding managers? I just want to get in my car and drive away." She winced before giving a small, surrendering smile. "But I guess I'll stand tall and stay."

He got that this was hard for her, and maybe she

was right. Maybe she should just jump in her car and forget the whole breakfast-with-the-Rawsons thing.

"Are you sure?" he asked.

A wave of red fell over her cheek as she nodded. "Except... I can't wear an evening dress or a man's shirt to your family's table."

"Well, I know how to fix that."

She was already onto it. "You mean contact Lanie and ask if she's got anything I can borrow."

Veda looked like she'd rather pull out her toenails.

"I can do it," he said.

"Thanks, but it'd seem less weird coming from me."

Just then his phone sounded. A text.

"Princess Lanie's morning ride must have taken her by here," he said, putting aside the phone after reading his sister's message.

Veda slumped. "She saw my car."

"She says that she just dropped off a selection of clothes at my front door, and she expects to see us both at breakfast." He cocked a brow. "Or else."

People openly talked about anxiety these days. No matter how infrequently, everyone experienced the sensations. Racing heartbeat. Increased blood flow. Feeling uneasy, flustered. Even panicked.

On her blog, Veda often addressed the issue. Her philosophy? Accept that you're only human and embrace the idea that you can work through it. Having grown up with a learning disability, a self-absorbed father and a mother who "loved too much," Veda felt as if she had earned the right to give advice on the subject.

As an adult, she continued to feel the fear and come out the other side, like last night when she'd been left alone to speak with Hux Rawson. Or now, walking into the Rawsons' dining room with Ajax as everyone's attention turned their way. Even the golden retriever lying by the closed porch door lifted its head to check her out. Just like last night with Hux, Veda's throat closed while her heart punched her ribs like a heavyweight champ. But she would get through it.

She always did.

The stunned silence ended when Lanie called out from a separate buffet table adorned with silver-domed platters.

"You guys want a coffee?" she asked. Her attitude was, *Nothing to see here, folks. Just my lady-killer brother with his latest conquest, who just happens to be my friend and a Darnel.*

As promised in the text, Lanie had left an assortment of clothes on Ajax's office doorstep; Veda had chosen a mustard-colored sundress and matching sandals. And yet as Lanie laid two brimming coffee cups in front of a pair of vacant chairs, she avoided Veda's gaze. Didn't so much as try to return the smile.

As if Veda hadn't felt awkward enough.

From his vantage point at the head of the massive table, Hux Rawson nodded a greeting as Veda and Ajax took their seats to his left. Brother Griff raised his cup and muttered, "Morning," while Jacob offered an easy smile, as did the beautiful woman beside him. A high chair sat between the pair, occupied by a little boy playing "squish" with a banana.

Veda expected Hux to rise above any perceived awkwardness and say something inclusive…welcoming. But he was looking off toward an adjoining doorway—perhaps the kitchen—as if someone had just called his name.

As relaxed and charming as ever, Ajax did the honors.

"Everyone, for those who don't know, this is Veda."

No surname supplied, which set off a tug-of-war in the pit of Veda's gut. She would rather Darnel wasn't mentioned, but like it or not, it was a big part of who she was.

Jacob was the first to speak up.

"I didn't get over to say hi last night. I'm Jacob." He ruffled the boy's mop of dark hair, an identical shade to his own. "This is my son, Buddy. And next to him, the other love of my life."

The woman's eyes sparkled with obvious affection for them both before she met Veda's gaze. "I'm Teagan. Great to meet you, Veda. Can I just say—I love your hair."

Veda had brought a small comb in her evening purse. Not nearly enough to get through this morning's whole new level of tangle. Then she had used Ajax's brush to sort through as many knots as she could, which still hadn't taken care of things.

Smiling, Veda ran two fingers around a thick wave. "There's lots of it, and it's all red."

The oldest Rawson brother introduced himself. "I'm Griff."

Veda returned his smile, which looked a little wooden.

"Nice to meet you, Griff," she said.

"Did you have a nice time last night, Veda?" Hux asked as Susan entered the room. Upon seeing the additional guest, she hesitated before recovering to take a seat alongside Hux.

"It was a lovely evening," Veda replied without a stumble, although her hands in her lap were clutched tight enough to strangle someone. "Just beautiful."

"I got to bed around three." Having set down her plate of hash browns and avocado toast, Lanie took her seat between Susan and Ajax at the same time she blew a kiss to her dad. "Positively the best night ever."

Susan was looking past Lanie and Ajax to Veda. "We discussed a song, you and I."

Veda nodded and smiled. Susan was such a sweet lady. "It's still doing rounds in my head."

Ajax finished swallowing a mouthful of coffee. "What song?"

Susan sang a couple of lines about creating a dream come true, and then winked at Hux while everyone else either chuckled or grinned. Veda felt her own smile warm her right through. Yes, this was awkward. She and Lanie would need to talk later. But the overall energy said *togetherness*…said family ties and lots of love.

When Ajax pushed back his chair and nodded toward the buffet table, Veda followed his lead and stood up. While she put some strawberries and a lemon muffin on her plate, Ajax gathered enough food to stock her refrigerator for a week. Meanwhile, at the table, the Rawsons were back to discussing the party. The focus was off her, thank God.

While taking their seats again, Hux kicked off a different conversation, speaking directly to Ajax.

"I've had an interesting chat with Yvette Maloney. She wants to buy a few acres that butt up against her property, and for an eye-popping price, I gotta say."

"You mean the parcel with the original house," Ajax said, squeezing a pool of ketchup onto his plate. "Not for sale."

"That old place needed a bulldozer when Dad was a kid," Griff said.

"Not anymore." Ajax collected his silverware. "I've done some work on it over the years."

Hux's eyebrows shot up. "Where'd you find the time?"

"A day here and there." Ajax cut into a fat sausage. "In my opinion, those acres are the best we have. Yvette Maloney knows that."

The men back-and-forthed for a while. When the subject ran out of steam, Jacob took a fork and pinged it against his glass.

"Everyone, I have an announcement to make."

Hux swallowed a mouthful of waffle. "We're all ears, son."

Jacob reached past the high chair to squeeze his partner's shoulder. "I gave Teagan a ring this morning." He caught her gaze and smiled like only a man in love could. "We've set a date."

The room erupted as everyone got to their feet to

give Teagan hugs while Buddy's plump cheeks pinked up with excitement and he slapped banana all over his bib. Veda remembered Lanie mentioning their situation. Jacob had been given full custody by Buddy's mother while Teagan—a billionaire's daughter, no less—was relatively new to such a family dynamic.

Veda didn't insert herself among the well-wishers. She simply smiled, letting the newly engaged couple know how happy she was for them both. The way they gazed at each other—with respect and pure adoration— it was clear they had a wonderful future ahead of them.

Suddenly the backs of Veda's eyes began to prickle. It happened sometimes when she thought about marriage. Kids. Of course all that was way down on her to-do list. Right now her focus was on her work and helping her Best Life Now clients achieve their goals. But one day she *would* like a family of her own.

And, boy oh boy, would she do it right.

Jacob reached across and lifted Teagan's left hand; a multi-carat emerald-cut diamond sparkled on her third finger. Standing behind the couple, Ajax glanced across the table and caught Veda's gaze. His brows nudged together and his head slanted before he returned his attention to the happy couple and their child.

"We'll need to celebrate," Susan said, drifting back to her seat. "An engagement party."

"My father wants to give us a party in Australia," Teagan said, mopping up banana from around Buddy's mouth. "You're all welcome, of course."

"A trip Down Under." Griff scratched his head. "What's that? A twenty-two-hour flight?"

"From this side of the country," Teagan replied. "I live in Seattle. Or *did* live there."

Jacob explained for Veda's sake. "Teagan's moved to Connecticut to be with Buddy and me."

There was more talk about the wedding, which would take place on the Rawson property, the same kind of elaborate party pavilion-style event as last night's birthday do. Veda thought about the distant future and the possibility of having a wedding at the Darnel estate. Her father was often so cynical and miserable, she couldn't see him offering his home, let alone being truly happy for her no matter who she married. Drake didn't believe in that kind of love.

Everyone returned to their seats and their various conversations. But Lanie still avoided Veda. Was her friend that taken aback at this turn of events between Ajax and Veda or was she simply annoyed?

Ajax was finishing the last of his hash browns when Griff caught his attention from the other side of the table.

"Ajax, you got a minute?"

Dabbing his mouth, Ajax looked Veda's way. She nodded. Of course he should go talk with his brother. It opened the door for her and Lanie to have a chat, which would include an explanation of how Ajax and she had first met. Simply put, she had fallen for Ajax Rawson's charms not once now, but twice. He made her feel so good. Like when they were alone, and in the zone, she didn't have to try.

Didn't have to think.

And, yes, she knew he'd made a lot of women feel that way.

Someone's phone was ringing. Hux pulled a device out of his top pocket and studied the caller ID with a quizzical look on his face.

Getting to his feet, Griff asked, "Who is it, Dad?"

"Matt Quibell. From the State Gaming Commission."

Veda didn't miss the look Griff slid Ajax's way before he said, "Maybe you should call him back."

But Hux was connecting the call. "Matt's a friend. He might want to congratulate us on yesterday's win."

Griff lowered himself back into his seat and motioned for Ajax to do the same as Hux Rawson swiped his phone screen to pick up. Lanie and Teagan talked across the table while Buddy sucked a piece of toast and Jacob looked between Griff and Ajax. Veda got that receiving a call from anyone at the Commission, particularly on a Sunday morning, was a big deal. But Hux had said this guy was a friend.

However, by the time Hux finished the call, with only a few mumbled words from his end, his face was gray. He dropped the phone on the table and fell back in his chair like he'd caught a bullet in the chest. Susan reached to hold his hand.

"What happened?" she asked. "Huxley, what's wrong?"

"Yesterday after the race, an objection was lodged regarding our runner in the twelfth," he said.

Ajax gave a slanted grin. "It was a dry track. A clean race."

"Matt wanted me to know the objection relates to allegations of horse doping." Hux's brows knitted as he eyeballed his son. "Those allegations, Ajax, are against you."

Ajax was lost for words.

He felt everyone's questions drilling into him and, holy shit, he had them, too. Overmedicating, doping... no question, it happened in the industry. But everyone knew that Ajax Rawson's horses won fair and square or not at all.

Shaking his head again, he tried to resurrect his smile, shake everything off, because this was crazier than purple snowflakes in June. It was crazy to think he would throw away his sterling reputation, and for what? A Grade 1 purse? Yes, his was a nice cut. But Rawson horses had won plenty and would win plenty more.

"That's a crock." Ajax scanned the table of shocked faces and shrugged. "It's a mistake."

Jacob asked their father, "Who made the allegation?" like he was already taking notes in his head for a legal defense.

"An assistant trainer." Hux was focused on Ajax. "He claims he saw your float driver, Paul Booshang, using a syringe."

Ajax heard Veda's sharp intake of air as he held up a hand. "Stop right there. Paul is a good guy. I trust him like everyone I allow near my horses. That assistant trainer is full of it."

"You left right after the usual samples were taken from Someone's Prince Charming," Hux said.

"Sure." Ajax shrugged. "I needed to get back for the party."

"Later, Booshang was questioned by a steward. Apparently he wanted to come clean. He said you'd done this kind of thing before. That you must've gotten away with false negatives in the past. Or you'd paid someone off."

Ajax's heart was pounding in his chest and in his ears. Gravity wanted to suck him back down into his seat. But he lifted his chin and stood firm, even as steam rose from around his collar. Even as his hands fisted into mallets by his sides.

"I need to talk to Paul." Now.

"Good luck finding him, because I'd bet my right leg he won't be anywhere around here." Hux threw his linen napkin on his plate. "Expect a call after the EDTP results are in."

Ajax heard Teagan ask Jacob in a near whisper, "What's EDTP?"

In a low voice, Jacob replied, "New York's Equine Drug Testing Program. Postrace testing is performed by Morrisville State College under contract with the Gaming Commission."

While Ajax digested the news, Hux looked somehow resigned. Or was that disappointed? Impossible. Ajax's ethics were as sound as his father's. Hux couldn't possibly believe...not for one second...

Ajax remembered Veda sitting beside him. She was gripping the edge of the table, looking up at him like he'd grown a pair of horns. Like he was already guilty as charged. And if for any reason those results came back positive for banned substances, as owner and trainer, he would be held legally responsible. Whether he was involved or not, the buck stopped with him.

Sitting forward, Griff clasped his hands on the table. "I don't think Booshang acted on his own."

"He's in this with someone else?" Jacob's amber-gold gaze burned into his brother's. "Why would you think that?"

Griff's jaw flexed. "I overhead something at the party last night."

Ajax's head snapped back. *My God*. "You knew this was coming, didn't you?"

That's why Griff had wanted to talk last night. Why he'd been so eager to get him away from the table a minute ago. He wanted a huddle before this all hit.

When he was thirteen, Griff had decided to befriend a stallion named Devil's Fire. Now he absently rubbed the scar above his left eye that had resulted from a secret bareback mount and subsequent fall.

"I caught a few words of a conversation between two guests you'd invited, Dad," Griff said. "One had a horse in the same race. I heard him say that a steward was speaking with one of our drivers who had links to…certain people."

Hux's voice rose. "Speak up, son. Links to who?"

Griff averted his gaze when he ground out, "Drake Darnel."

As blood drained from his head, Ajax shut his eyes. Booshang had worked for other stables in the past, in-

cluding Darnel's. Obviously he hadn't held it against
the guy. But now Ajax was boiling mad inside. Not
only had Booshang abused his trust on so many levels,
now Drake Darnel was involved? Was he that jealous
of Rawson's impeccable reputation and list of wins that
he would try to frame them? Or was this some warped
form of revenge for Hux supposedly stealing Drake's
girl all those years ago?

Like, seriously—get a life!

Ajax strode for the door. "I'm going to find
Booshang, wherever the hell he is, and tell him he's
got two choices. Talk, and fast, or—"

"Being a hothead won't solve anything," Jacob said,
shooting to his feet. "We need some kind of strategy
going forward."

Ajax took a breath. When Jacob had first arrived at
the farm all those years ago, Ajax had been less than
taken with the juvie kid from Brooklyn. Jacob had been
defensive, on the edge. But Hux had seen something in
the troubled teen. Jacob had had to work to gain their
father's trust but, hey, hadn't they all?

Hux pushed back his chair. "Let's get on it then.
We'll need vet records for a start. And a detective to
dig around and see if there's anything to a Darnel connection." He squeezed Susan's hand before he stood
and nodded toward his den at the back of the house.
"Giddyap, boys."

When Ajax saw Jacob ruffling his son's hair and
kissing his fiancée, he remembered Veda again. He
strode back over and took her hand. Hux's dog, Ches-

ter, scrambled out of the way as Ajax swung open the door and ushered Veda outside onto the porch.

"And you thought this wasn't going to be easy," he joked as he shut the connecting door for privacy's sake.

Releasing his hand, Veda continued to give him an unimpressed look.

"I need to go."

Ajax couldn't argue. He had business to take care of, no getting around that. And, irrespective of whether her nutjob father was actually involved in this mess, now Veda needed some time and space.

"I'll walk you down to your car."

"I can walk myself." Her stony mask eased a little. "I wanted to talk to Lanie, but that can wait."

What a mess. This morning couldn't have ended worse. "I'm sorry this happened."

"It's almost poetic justice, don't you think?"

"Meaning…?"

"You and I…not the best idea."

His chest tightened, but he managed a stoic smile. "Let me sort this out."

When he took her hands, she pulled away.

"Do what you need to do. I don't want to be involved."

He held her gaze. "Just so we're clear, I don't dope my horses."

"You mean with steroids? Or just with too much of the legal stuff? Everyone knows it happens, and way more than the establishment cares to admit. No one even talks about the jockeys' lives that are put at risk when a juiced-up horse breaks down."

Ajax shot back, "In case you missed it, your father could be implicated." Her comment stung, and he couldn't help himself.

"Go ahead and join the dots for me." She crossed her arms. "I know you want to."

"Booshang worked at Darnel Stables in the past. Given how much your father hates Hux, maybe it's a frame job."

"Why would Booshang risk his job and a fine to help set you up?"

"Geez, I don't know. Maybe *money*? Your father is loaded. And he still has it out for Hux. Poor jealous bastard."

When her eyes flashed and nostrils flared, Ajax knew he'd gone too far.

"I need the entry code to get into the office building," she said.

To get her belongings. He'd left his private suite unlocked, so fine.

But then Ajax paused. He couldn't be sure if Booshang was indeed still on Drake's payroll. Regardless, Veda wasn't involved. And the vast majority of his records were electronic. But if he allowed her unsupervised access to his office, to his hard files, would she be tempted to snoop? Not that she would find anything untoward. And he had cameras installed outside so he could check the footage later if need be.

He passed on the code and watched her stride off, red hair swishing, before he kicked a porch post as hard as he could. But he had to focus on his number one priority now. He needed to clear his name, and if that meant taking down Drake Darnel as an accomplice in this lie...

Ring the bell.

Bring it on.

Veda felt as if she had escaped a war zone. Breakfast with the Rawsons was supposed to have been a little shaky but ultimately fine. She should never have agreed to go. She should never have gotten with Ajax again, full stop. For whatever reason—and there were a few—it was always going to end badly.

She took a shortcut to the Rawson office through a lush connecting paddock. Inhaling fresh air mixed with the smell of horse, she held each of her cheeks in turn, trying to pat away the heat. She had no prior knowledge of this doping incident. As for her father? Drake hated the Rawsons, but he wouldn't stoop to criminal behavior to discredit them. Absolutely not.

The Rawsons were the ones incriminated here, not the Darnels.

As for Booshang being the one at the heart of this matter...she wasn't about to blurt out her personal association with Paul in front of Ajax or anyone else; how suspicious would that look? She didn't know whether Ajax had worked with Booshang to dope that horse, whether he'd done it before, and she didn't *want* to know. As far as she was concerned, this was the end. Ajax could send as many flowers as he liked. He could call her until his redial finger dropped off. She would never buckle and see him again.

She couldn't get out of here fast enough.

Using the code, Veda let herself into the building. She grabbed her gown, shoes and purse and headed for the door again. But then a series of glaring thoughts stopped her dead.

Ajax's denial of involvement had seemed genuine, but if he *was* involved, she doubted he would simply throw up his hands and confess, particularly in front of his family. His father. Could Paul Booshang prove Ajax's involvement? Might there be some kind of evidence hidden away within these walls? A signed contract between the two men, maybe? But where would a person begin to look? If she dared, how much might she find?

Veda's ears pricked up. Through the open door, she heard a dog bark and hooves galloping nearer. She hurried out.

On the back of a magnificent black Thoroughbred, Lanie was closing the distance between them, her long dark hair streaming behind her.

Lanie had been kind enough to lend her these clothes. Her friend had also offered a welcoming comment when she and Ajax had entered the Rawsons' dining room earlier, but she hadn't met Veda's gaze once. Obviously she wasn't happy about her friend's overnight arrangements. How much less impressed would Lanie be when she found out that this wasn't the first time?

With an armful of red evening gown, Veda was opening her car door when Lanie jumped out of her saddle.

"I thought you and I should talk," she said, tossing

the reins over a rail as the Rawsons' golden retriever scooted to a stop on her heels.

"This isn't the best time," Veda said, dumping her belongings on the back seat.

"You stayed with Ajax last night." She was stroking her horse's neck. "I had assumed he wasn't your type."

"But then Ajax is every girl's type, right?"

Lanie's hand dropped. "Who exactly are you angry with?"

"I'm angry with myself."

"Because you made a mistake?"

"Because I made *two*." When Lanie's eyebrows shot up, Veda slammed the door shut. "Don't look at me like that."

"Well, see, here's the funny part. Early last night, I caught him looking at you like a wolf might drool over a juicy lamb chop. I told him you were off-limits."

So Lanie had been looking out for her, defending her from her stud brother, while Veda had lied to her friend by omission.

Veda slumped back against the car. "I should have told you."

"You don't owe me an explanation. Women find my brother exceedingly attractive—irresistible, in fact—and he knows it."

"That makes me feel so much better."

"As long as the two parties involved are consenting adults who know the stakes, it's off to the races, as they say."

Veda opened the driver's-side door. "I don't intend to see him again."

"Because of this doping business?"

"Among other things."

"Playing hard to get will only make him chase you more."

Veda sank in behind the wheel. "I'm not playing."

The glint in Lanie's bright blue gaze softened. "You're my friend, no matter what happens between you and Ajax. And remember... I'm his sister, not his keeper. I don't control what he does, how he feels. No one does." Lanie shrugged. "And who knows? Maybe in you, the mighty Ajax will finally meet his match."

Veda was buckling her seat belt. "Don't be facetious."

"I'm serious. Although if it's proven that your dad is behind this doping plot..."

"My father is *not* involved."

Lanie's smile was wry. "For everyone's sake, I hope not."

As Lanie rode off over the hill, Veda counted to ten. She liked Lanie but she didn't like the conversation they'd just had. It brought back memories of her first-grade teacher, and others, telling her that she needed to be smarter. Try harder. It made her feel like she wasn't sure about their friendship anymore.

Like maybe all the Rawsons were more trouble than they were worth.

Seven

Ajax got to his feet as Veda made her way through the sea of round tables set up for the Best Life Now "Motivation Is Key" seminar.

"Surprise," he said as she jolted to a dead stop in front of him.

Veda's eyes were wide and her mouth was hanging open like she'd just seen the ghost of lovers past. Two weeks had gone by since Lanie's party, which had ended with him and Veda enjoying one hell of a reunion. While he hadn't phoned or sent flowers, he hadn't forgotten her. Along with the pain-in-the-butt doping scandal that hadn't found a resolution yet, Veda had been at the forefront of his mind, particularly when he lay in bed at night. It would have driven him nuts if he hadn't come up with this plan B.

Veda's presentation had ended ten minutes ago. While she had spoken with interested attendees who wanted to personally introduce themselves, the majority of the audience had left the room. Now Veda flickered a glance around, taking in the stragglers while running a palm down the side of her emerald-green pantsuit.

"What are you doing here?" she asked in a hushed, harried tone.

"You invited me," Ajax explained.

Her eyes widened again as she hissed, "I so did not invite you."

"You said I ought to come along to one of your seminars. I looked up your website, saw this gig, in beautiful Barbados no less, and ta-da!" He held out his hands. "Here I am."

Her chest rose and fell a few more times before she returned a smile laced with venom. "Well, I hope you found my talk enlightening. Now, if you'll excuse me…"

As she breezed past him and through one of the opened doors, Ajax drank in the vision of her swaying hips before he nodded goodbye to the kind and still curious ladies who had allowed him to join their table when he had arrived halfway through Veda's talk.

"If you're through for the day," he said, catching up, "I thought we could have a drink."

Veda smiled at attendees who nodded and waved at the same time she cut Ajax a response.

"I think not."

"Veda, we need to talk."

She hitched the strap of her carryall higher on her shoulder. "Nothing to discuss."

"You're not curious about the horse doping thing?"

Her step faltered before she strode on, chin even higher. "Not curious enough to get involved."

When they had spoken last, he'd said Booshang might be on the take with her father offering the bribe. He still had no proof of that, and there'd been some kind of delay with the test results. He only knew that given Drake's grudge, a conspiracy theory fit, and his family agreed.

Veda pushed open another door. Ajax was ready to follow her inside until the restroom sign stopped him dead.

Five or so minutes later, Veda emerged from the women's bathroom and strode past again, this time heading for the elevators. If she got inside, that was his cutoff point. He'd come here to talk, not to flat-out stalk. He was slowing his pace, backing off, when she ducked behind a huge framed poster set up in a largely unpopulated corner of the lobby. Then her arm slid out and a curling finger beckoned him over. Ajax darted a look around, wondering if this was some kind of trap, and joined her.

"I'll be clear," she said. "Ajax, I don't want to see you again."

Given the circumstances under which they had parted, he'd expected that. Now was the time to lay all his cards on the table. No holding back.

"I came here in person to let you know face-to-face how I feel about you. How I feel about *us*."

She looked unmoved. "I already know how you feel. You think we're good in bed."

"We aren't *good* in bed, Veda. We're *phenomenal*."

"Like you haven't said that to a woman before."

"I know you feel it, too," he said, ignoring that last dig. "Maybe it's because we both grew up in families who own stables. Or maybe because we're opposites in lots of ways, and opposites are meant to attract."

"Sometimes they repel. Like water and really oily slime."

He wouldn't take offense. "That's not how this is." He edged closer. "That's not you and me."

She hesitated like he might be getting through, but then she straightened and seemed to shake it off. "It doesn't matter that we share an attraction."

Damn it. "The point is I miss you. And I think you miss me."

When she didn't try to deny it, Ajax felt pressure as well as relief. Taking in every beautiful inch of her face—apple cheeks, cute nose and lips that were parted the barest amount—he knew this was the moment to act. So he set a palm against the wall near her head and oh so carefully leaned in. When he thought she might surrender, before he could actually connect, she dodged under his arm and was gone.

But when he emerged from their hidey-hole behind the poster, he found that she hadn't run away. Her expression wasn't *I'm yours*, but she didn't look like she wanted his balls on a chopping block anymore, either.

She adjusted her bag strap again and conceded, "I guess…now that you're here…"

Ajax tried to hide his grin when he prodded.
"Yes, Veda?"

She blew out a resigned breath. "Well, I guess you can buy me one drink."

While they found a table in an open-air bar with a spectacular view of the ocean, Veda told herself to calm the heck down. Her hands wanted to shake. Her heart was pumping like a steam train piston. After two weeks with no word, she had assumed Ajax had lost interest. Which had hurt—a lot—but was better than the alternative, which entailed finding the wherewithal not to answer if he called.

She'd been beyond shocked—and pissed—that he had taken it upon himself to show up at this exclusive seminar out of the blue. How rude. How presumptuous. On the other hand, yes, she was also a teeny bit flattered. He had obviously been thinking about her, and God knows she'd been thinking about him, too… in more ways than one.

"So, you really don't want to know what's happening with that ridiculous doping allegation?" Ajax asked, like he'd read her mind.

"Let me guess." Sitting across from him, she inhaled the fresh, beach-scented air and set her bag down. "Your lawyer brother hasn't found any link to my father."

The gleam in his eyes said *not yet.* "Although Drake was happy to make a comment to the press when asked."

"Unfavorable, I suppose."

"You could say that." He sat back, looking like a dream in a shirt the same color as the water, a light breeze combing through his hair. "Jacob has tried to speak with Booshang. He's not cooperating."

"Which doesn't let you off the hook."

Paul Booshang had implicated Ajax, but he had worked for the Darnel Stables in the past, when she was a girl. Back then, if her father had ever found out that Paul was up to no good, he'd have been out on his ear.

Then again, Drake didn't know everything, did he?

"So I presume the results were positive," she said.

"They haven't come back yet. Some kind of delay at the lab. In the meantime, Jacob has his people digging around, trying to get to the bottom of it all. Other than Booshang's claim that I organized the whole deal, there's not a shred of evidence."

"Or evidence to the contrary."

"And thanks for the continued vote of confidence."

Her smile was tight. "You're welcome."

An impeccably dressed waiter appeared, setting down the drinks as Ajax asked, "Have you spoken to your father?"

"I dropped in before driving home that morning. Word travels fast in the racing industry. He'd already heard."

"And he asked you to pass on his best wishes, right?"

"Actually, he said that he'd always known this kind of thing would come out."

"Particularly if he helped set us up."

She stirred her creamy mocktail with her straw.

"When you find out that my father had nothing to do with this, I'll accept your apology."

"I'll look forward to his apology as well."

That would never happen. Never in a hundred years. In a million.

"So have you and Lanie spoken?" he asked, changing the subject as he picked up his glass.

Veda remembered their talk outside the Rawsons' office building that morning.

"She said whatever happened between us was our business. But she wasn't exactly cheering from the sidelines. She said she is in no way responsible for your behavior."

He paused before setting his beer back down. "I don't need to defend myself."

"Then don't."

He got back on point. "I care about you, Veda. I wouldn't be here if I didn't."

Veda remembered Lanie's parting remark about her being the one who might bring the mighty Ajax Rawson down. Before that, Lanie had said that playing hard to get would only make Ajax more determined to see her again. She hadn't been playing, and yet here he was.

Which raised an obvious question.

"You must have pursued other women," she said, stirring her drink some more.

"The point is I'm pursuing *you*. Pursuing *us*."

With those seductive blue eyes smiling into hers, he looked so convincing. But if Lanie was right, Ajax's relationships were largely about the chase. Veda had been putty in his hands the first time; she'd been won over the second. If she gave in a third time *and* let him think that she was seriously falling for him, would the Stud pull back on his reins? If she upped the ante and said she wanted a future together, would he turn tail and run?

Pursuing him rather than the other way around was an insane idea. Even dangerous as far as her heart was concerned. But now she couldn't help but wonder.

Ajax cared about her?

Exactly how much, and for how long?

"The seminar's organizers are putting on a dinner tonight," she said, really curious now. "I can take someone."

His eyebrows shot up. "You're asking me?"

"You want to spend time together, right?"

"Right. Except…"

Except, suddenly this was too easy?

"You don't want to come?" she asked, feeling bolder now.

He gave her a smoldering, lopsided grin. "Of course I want to come."

Veda's stomach jumped before she manufactured an encouraging smile.

"So, dinner tonight?"

His cocky grin widened. "It just so happens that I'm free."

Eight

Ajax finished fastening the Tiffany cuff links before swinging the formal jacket off its hanger and slotting his arms into the sleeves. Standing before his hotel suite's full-length mirror, he ran his fingers through his shower-damp hair, then blew out a long breath.

To the starting gates, boys.

Following Veda here to Barbados had seemed like a no-brainer. It was either make a big gesture or continue to have her sail right out of his life. He couldn't let that happen. Not without giving it his all. But he hadn't thought that getting her back would be this, well, easy.

As he sat on the edge of the bed, slipping his feet in his shoes, Ajax remembered how he'd imagined Veda's initial reaction: shock followed by a flip of the bird. He'd been stoked when she caved and agreed to a drink instead. Tying the first shoelace, he recalled how she'd warmed up more at the bar. Not only had she agreed to see him again, she'd invited him to this dinner. It had crossed his mind to suggest that she come up to his room beforehand, because by that time, he'd gotten the impression she wouldn't say no.

Pulling the second shoelace taut, it snapped right off in his hand. Ajax tossed the piece aside and got on the phone to the concierge.

"Strange request. I need a shoelace," he said as his gaze landed on the king-size bed. He imagined Veda lying there naked among the cushions, calling him over, and couldn't they please stay the whole week?

The concierge was saying it could take up to thirty minutes to have a shoelace delivered.

"I'll come down and grab one. Thanks."

This would be a good night, Ajax reaffirmed to himself as he left the room with one loose shoe. Better than their night in Saratoga. Even better than after Lanie's birthday party.

And tomorrow morning…?

The elevator doors slid open. After stepping inside, he dug his socked toes into that loose shoe while visualizing the most obvious outcome. Tomorrow morning they would make love for the third or fourth time since returning from dinner. Then they would talk, probably about setting a date to see each other again.

But he was snowed under at the moment. It didn't make things easier that Hux had been weird since that phone call from his pal at the Commission. And Drake's recent comments to the press questioning the legitimacy of Rawson's long list of wins certainly didn't help.

For years, his father had left the majority of business decisions to Ajax. These past couple of weeks, however, Hux was always in the office or hanging around the stables. Asking questions. Going over things. Once he'd even enquired about Veda, and not in a supportive way.

When Ajax left the elevator, he finally lost the unlaced shoe. Picking it up, he continued across the extensive lobby floor. He didn't want to think about that other situation back home now. He wanted to focus on Veda because he absolutely couldn't wait to see her again. The thought of her made him buzz all over, like his blood was vibrating, it was pumping that hard.

Sure, he liked playing the field, like Griff. And, yes, like their father when he was younger, although that had changed when Hux had met "the one." Apparently, back then, Ajax's mom had let her future husband know early on that she wasn't letting go. Hux said that after a couple of dates he had known it would be until death do us part.

Gripping that shoe, Ajax shivered to his bones. Committing to a woman for life was one thing. Having her taken away far too soon was something else again. Losing his sweetheart had broken Hux in two. Ajax had never contemplated testing fate the same way. He had never imagined himself, well…risking that much.

One lousy misstep and everything could be lost.

A man behind the reception desk ambled over. After Ajax had explained about the shoelace, the clerk went off to hunt one down and Ajax's thoughts returned to Veda. When he'd texted earlier, she'd said they should meet here in the lobby. He smiled to himself wondering what she would be wearing? The lipstick-red number was a hard one to beat, but then Veda looked amazing no matter what she had on. In fact, his favorite getup had to be that oversize men's shirt and black cowboy hat.

What man in his right mind would pass that up? Who wouldn't want to grab on and never let go?

Still holding the shoe, Ajax crossed his arms and exhaled. What a night that had been. It made him wonder how this evening would compare. Guess he'd find out soon enough.

And in the morning...

Tomorrow morning...

Leaving the elevators, Veda saw him standing by the front desk—holding a shoe?

Ajax looked particularly gorgeous in a dark blue suit that accentuated those beautiful broad shoulders all the way down his long, strong legs. But his usual cheeky grin was nowhere to be seen. In fact, his eyebrows were drawn together and his freshly shaved jaw was thrust forward.

She couldn't have anticipated Ajax showing up uninvited, for all intents and purposes, at the seminar. The bigger shock was her asking him—and in record time—to be her date for this evening's dinner. But she was determined to go through with her plan. Either way, this had to end. Better it be sooner rather than later and with her in the driver's seat.

Following Lanie Rawson's insider opinion, when a woman pursued Ajax rather than the other way around, he lost interest. This class of male was all about the chase. When she fully leaned in to grab Ajax's charms with both hands—when she let him think that she was ready to be his happily-ever-after—he would choke and retreat. Problem solved.

Of course, in order for this plan to play out, she would need to end up in his bed again. She wouldn't complain. Nor would she hold back. Tonight she had a valid reason to really let loose. In the afterglow, she would bring up the possibility of marriage.

Come tomorrow morning, Ajax Rawson would be running for the hills.

After a uniformed man behind the desk passed something over to Ajax, he took a seat in the lobby lounge. Now she could see that he was rethreading his shoe with a new lace. Drawing nearer, Veda watched the jacket stretch taut across his broad back as he worked. Even doing such a mundane chore, his moves were close to hypnotic.

She was closing the distance, almost upon him, when he looked up and sent over the slowest, sexiest smile. Veda flushed—cheeks, breasts. *Everything.*

As he got to his feet, she put her plan in motion, giving him an openly salacious once-over. When his smile faltered, she read his thoughts. *What exactly is going on here?* he was wondering. Then she stepped into the space separating them, set her hand on his lapel, pushed up on tiptoe and brushed her lips over the fine-sandpaper feel of his jaw.

"God, you look hot," she murmured near his ear.

When she pulled back, she could barely contain her grin. Ajax looked shell-shocked. It would sting like hell when this ended, but in the meantime she was good with having an obscene amount of fun. Call it payback for all the girls who had been left behind in the Stud's wake.

He cleared his throat, resumed that dynamite smile and acknowledged her dress—a sheath made from a shimmering Caribbean print fabric with a corset back. She had planned to wear a matching cap-sleeved bolero jacket, but in this case, less was definitely more.

"And you look absolutely beautiful," he said. "Breathtaking, in fact."

Playing it up, she glanced down at her bust. "You don't think it's too...snug?"

She had laced herself up extra tight to get the maximum advantage from her cleavage.

"Not too snug," he assured her. "Just right."

She glanced down at his feet. "You had some kind of problem?"

"Would you believe I threw a shoe. All fixed now, though." He stomped like a horse and then offered her his arm. "Shall we?" As they walked to the elevators, she was aware of heads turning, men's as well as women's. Aside from looking like Hollywood's top leading man, Ajax oozed charisma and smelled divine. This might not end well, but right now it felt good to be the one on his arm.

A woman joined them in the elevator going up. Her bobbed honey-blond hair and black evening gown with its halter neckline made for a stunning combination. But all of Ajax's attention was focused on his date. On Veda. Given the famished look in his eyes, she wondered whether he might tell her there was a change of plans. That he was taking her straight up to his room and staying there.

When the doors slid open, Veda let out her breath. She'd been full of confidence earlier, but he was the one with all the experience. Had she bitten off more than she could chew?

They followed the woman out and headed toward the ballroom's open doors.

"I've already told you how beautiful you look, haven't I?" he asked in a voice that suddenly sounded deeper and slightly rougher.

She pressed a palm against her stomach to ease her nerves. "Breathtaking, you said, and not too snug."

"You smell beautiful, too," he said as they entered the room. "What is that? Something French?"

"It's domestic." And hardly expensive.

"Want to know something?"

He looked so intense and sincere, like he had a juicy big secret he needed to share. She smiled, nodded. "Sure."

"I want to thank you."

"Thank me for what?"

"For trusting me. For not walking away."

It was on the tip of her tongue…snide and a little bitter. *Has any woman ever walked away, Ajax?* But tonight was all about an experiment that had only one logical conclusion. She would continue to come on to him, strong and relentless, and be the victor when she scared him away.

Throughout the evening, Ajax tried to look interested. And he had to admit, there were some high points. Like the main course, which featured the freshest lobster on earth. Veda seemed happy with her vegetarian option. He guessed tofu actually worked for some palates.

The conversation around the table was…interesting. Their dinner companions were well-heeled folks involved in the self-help business. There was a psychologist guru and his wife, a personal budget planning person and her high-profile chiropractor partner. The rest were people who had enjoyed being part of the exclusive seminar audience today.

While awards for best this and most acclaimed that were presented, Ajax tried to remain present. Rather than let his mind wander to the challenges that awaited him back home, he focused on Veda. Along with that dress, which was stimulation enough, she was doing all kinds of suggestive things, like when she'd held his eyes while licking her dessert spoon real slow and all around. Or when she'd "accidentally" missed her mouth and spilled water between her spectacular cleavage. Either Veda was trying hard to let him know something or he was losing his grip.

A waiter was removing their dessert plates when Veda settled her hand high on his thigh. And squeezed.

Ajax slid her a pointed look while what was behind his zipper paid attention, too.

"I guess you're ready to go then?" he asked as her nails circled, then slid higher.

Her smile said, *You'd better believe it.*

He was pushing back his chair when she said, "I need to have a word with someone first. I won't be long. Can you wait a couple of minutes?"

He scooted his chair back in. A couple of minutes? Sure. "I'll be here."

He watched her weave between the tables and people milling about, some leaving, others heading for the dance floor. He would have liked a cheek-to-cheek but she was obviously keen to slide into home base. Which, of course, ratcheted up his anticipation levels. Because this was a sure bet.

Like really, *really* sure.

"Excuse me. I saw you earlier in the elevator."

He focused on the woman standing by his chair. "Oh," he said. "Hi."

"But I feel as if I've seen you before that," she went on.

He smiled. Shrugged. "I'm not sure."

She took Veda's vacant chair. "Maybe in a movie or a magazine."

Ajax chuckled. "Afraid not."

"Perhaps I've seen you at a previous event."

"This is a first for me."

Ajax flicked a glance Veda's way. She was deep in conversation with a couple on the other side of the room.

"The woman you're with…"

He replied, "Veda Darnel from Best Life Now. She spoke today."

She glanced at his left hand. "You two aren't married."

He shook his head. Definitely not married. "Veda and I are…good friends."

Her eyes suddenly rounded. "Oh, now I know where I've seen you before. You're Ajax Rawson. The Stud."

Ajax gave a wry grin. Would he ever live that tag down?

"I'm Ajax. Right."

"You own a big ranch. A stable." She sighed. "I love horses. I went to the Kentucky Derby last year. What an amazing day."

He paused, then turned a little toward her. "We lost by a nose last year." He mentioned the name of the horse.

"Oh, so close!" she agreed before arching a brow. "So which Rawson ride should I keep an eye out for next?"

"Actually, I have a good tip for the Breeders' Cup."

"So hopefully an Eclipse Award, too."

He looked Veda's way again. She was still talking. So he settled back and continued to share his tips.

When Veda turned back toward the table, her stomach dropped. Her falling-all-over-Ajax plan was working better, and faster, than she had even hoped. He was talking with a woman—the same woman who had shared the elevator ride from the lobby up to this floor—and looking more animated than he had all night. Like this woman was so entertaining, he couldn't get enough of her conversation. Like he was already over Veda after she'd lavished attention on him.

With measured steps, she approached their table and, gritting her teeth, joined them. It took a second for Ajax to realize she was there.

"Oh. Veda. This is Charlotte."

Charlotte continued to smile into Ajax's eyes and explain for Veda's benefit, "I'm a huge horse racing fan."

Perfect.

As Veda collected her purse off the table, Ajax got to his feet. "Did you catch up with your friends?"

"I did." Veda exhaled. "I think I'm done here."

When Charlotte got to her feet, too, Veda fought the urge to push her back down. "Please," she said. "Keep talking."

Charlotte tipped her head Ajax's way. "Your call."

Ajax actually took a moment before he replied. "It was great meeting you. Might see you at the Derby one year."

As Charlotte took her leave, Ajax reached to take Veda's hand. She stepped away. Frankly, she wanted to kick his shin. Lanie was right about her brother in spades. All about the chase.

"I really don't want to get in the way," she said, overly sweet.

He had the audacity to look confused. "What...you mean get in the way of me and that woman?" His grin was pure charm. "I met her two minutes ago."

"Well, you do work fast."

His look said *you've lost a screw.* Like she was

cranking the crazy for believing her eyes, knowing
his record the way she did. Her plan tonight had been
to come on so strong that he lost interest. But now she
wondered. Would he have flirted with that woman regardless?

"Veda," he said calmly, sincerely, "she came over
and recognized me. I was filling in time, waiting for
you."

As she studied those blue, blue eyes, her throat
began to close. Irrespective of whether that was true,
she felt like a loser. Like a lost, misunderstood teen-
ager again.

She blew out a shaky breath. "Ajax... You do my
head in."

He kept his gaze on hers, looking as if, for once,
he didn't know what to say. It was her move to make,
and she knew what to do. What she should have done
when he'd shown up unannounced earlier.

She walked away.

"I'm going to bed," she said, and then added, "*alone.*"

An hour later, she had changed into her pj's and was
staring blindly out over the quiet moonlit waters, feeling lower than low, when she heard a knock. Knowing
who it was, she walked to the door, opened up. Ajax
stood there, his tie hanging loose, shirt half-undone,
making *remorseful* look so sexy that she quivered.

"I'm sorry I hurt you," he said. "I honestly didn't
mean to."

While her heart continued to break, she took a long,
agonizing moment and finally stepped aside.

He crossed the threshold and, before the door had

even swung shut, somehow she was back in his arms, both hating and consoling herself for wanting this man more than ever.

After Veda had left him in that ballroom, Ajax went down to the bar and thought the whole thing through over a double scotch. She'd been open about her feelings and insecurities where his dating history was concerned. Talking to that woman... He hadn't done anything wrong. But, hey, he got where Veda was coming from.

He could see, he supposed, why she'd been upset.

Finally, he'd knocked back that scotch and then knocked on her door. After his apology, she had buckled and let him in. As soon as their lips touched, she melted in his arms. And as the kiss deepened and he brought her closer, he felt a tremor run through her as if she was feeling the same relief that he did.

"I didn't want you to come back," she said against his lips. "I prayed you wouldn't because I knew I'd give in."

His hold on her shoulders tightened as his gut clenched. "Veda...don't you know how much I care about you?"

She cupped his cheek and almost smiled. "You should show me."

Ajax slipped the tie from his collar and let it fall on the floor. Veda wasn't asking for sex. She wanted him to make love to her. She needed to know she wasn't just one in a line. Now he needed to know that, too.

As she led him into the bedroom, he took a quick

inventory…muted light, turned down bed. Then he held her face with both hands before brushing his lips over hers, feathering kisses on each side of her mouth until her eyes drifted shut and her hands covered his. Then he kissed her more deeply, but not the way he had at the door.

He stroked and teased her tongue with his, every now and then adjusting the angle and taking as much time as he could. When his lips finally left hers, her breathing was heavy and he was aching to move things along. But this wouldn't be like the last time when he'd jumped off that cliff way too early. He wanted to arouse her to the point of begging, then leave her satisfied beyond ever needing to question again.

He coaxed her around until her shoulder blades rested against his chest. After sweeping her hair to one side, he nuzzled a trail up the slope of her neck while his palm skimmed up and down over her pajama top. Nibbling her lobe, he undid three buttons and then slipped his hand in under the silk.

When Veda sucked in a breath, he shifted to rest his cheek against hers and slid his other hand into the opening, too. Veda's head fell back against his shoulder as she trembled and sighed. And when she pressed her behind against his thighs and undid the rest of the buttons herself, he coaxed her around to face him and kissed her again.

He blindly stepped her back until her legs met the bed. Then, easing the silk off her shoulders, he kissed her a little harder. When the sleeves caught at her elbows, he guided her down until she sat on the bed's edge. Lowering onto his knees, he drew one nipple into his mouth while she held on to his head, grazing the back of his leg with her toes.

"Take your shirt off, Veda," he said sometime later. "Honey, lie back flat on the bed."

Getting to his feet, he ditched the shirt and belt while taking in the picture of her doing as he'd asked. Her hair was a burnished halo. Her expression said, *I want to please as much as be pleased.* Leaning over her, one arm bracing his weight, he hooked three fingers into the waistband of her shorts and, little by little, tugged them down. Dropping the shorts by his feet, he studied that part of her he ached to know again.

Taking his time, he trailed a fingertip over her smooth, warm mound before tracing a teasing line down the center and between her thighs. Then, kneeling on the floor again, he caught her ankles and set her feet on the mattress. Savoring her sweet, heady scent, he used his thumbs to part and expose her further.

When he finally went down, she held his head while he stroked her with his tongue and slipped two fingers inside. It wasn't nearly long enough before she was gripping his ears, beginning to tremble. And as he reluctantly drew away, she held out her hand.

"Where are you going?"

He showed her the foil wrap he'd retrieved from his wallet before tossing it on the bed and ditching his clothes. When he stood before her again, she sat up and immediately coiled her fingers around the base of his shaft. Ajax groaned at the rush of heat as she angled him toward her mouth and ran her tongue around the tip three times. When she gripped his thigh, Ajax closed his eyes as, shifting forward and back, he cupped and held her moving jaw.

Before he got too close to that edge, he eased away and saw to the condom. He thought about swinging her on top of him but instead went the more traditional route. As she reached to link her arms around his neck, he positioned himself on top and eased inside…a long, deliberate stroke that felt like it lasted forever. Then he covered her mouth with his, matching the rhythm of the kiss to his thrusts.

When he thought she might be close again, he murmured a warning against her lips. "I wouldn't count on much sleep tonight."

On the brink, she grinned as she asked, "So what about the morning?"

He wanted to answer that question but he only picked up the pace.

Now just wasn't the time.

Nine

For as long as Ajax could remember, he was always up with the birds. And yet catching the time on his watch now—

Really? Was it after eight?

On any other day, he would be wrapping up track work and thinking ahead to checking on his foaling mares and attending to the books. But this morning he was with Veda. Although she was obviously already awake.

Ajax rubbed each eye and looked around the palatial plantation-style bedroom until his focus landed on the open door of the vast marble bathroom. Veda stood with her back to him, brushing out those gorgeous red waves. She was dressed in a romper that showed off her legs and was perfect for this setting. While relaxed, the resort was known for its luxury and pampering. Its facilities included three golf courses, a dozen spa treatment rooms, each with its own garden and plunge pool, and a massive, multi-layered swimming pool surrounded by coral-rock walls. There was plenty to do.

Right now Ajax was only interested in private pursuits.

As he pushed up on an elbow, every cell in his body told him he needed to get Veda back here in this bed. And later, when she wanted to talk about walking out on him after dinner last night, he'd happily listen.

She stopped brushing her hair midstroke and turned around. Finding his gaze, her expression stilled before a soft smile touched her lips and she headed back into the bedroom.

"Morning," she said.

"Morning back."

Getting ready for her to join him, he readjusted his position, sitting forward, resting his forearms on raised knees and lacing his fingers between his legs. But she crossed to the wardrobe instead, finding sandals to slip on her feet. Then she went through her open suitcase. Was she searching for sunscreen? A hat?

Or was she just filling in time?

"You're ahead of me this morning," he said, combing a hand through his bed hair.

"You should see the sky. So blue, it's unreal. The water, too."

Her tone matched his—light and easy. Which was in stark contrast to the intensity of their bedroom marathon the night before. And when she continued to fluff around in her suitcase and the silence got awkward, Ajax's thoughts returned to the previous day when he had wondered how things would be between them *this* particular morning after the night before.

Yesterday she had gone from *please disappear* to *I'm totally yours* in ten minutes flat. And she had continued in that steamy vein until that woman, Charlotte whoever, had sat down with him to share an innocent chat.

Veda had a thing about his "reputation." She didn't trust him. Apparently not for a New York minute. He had hoped that the time they'd spent together here last night would help, but now he wasn't getting that vibe.

As he got out of bed to pull on his pants, she wandered out onto the furnished terrace. When he joined her, he was taken aback by the view of golden sand and, farther out, turquoise water scattered with diamond drops of sunshine.

"I love the hills back home," he said, breathing in the warm salty air. "But this is pretty darn special."

"It's supposed to be hot today," she said, gazing out, too. "But I don't feel it. I think it'll be pretty mild."

He studied her profile, the small straight nose, elevated chin, determined green eyes that were sparkling as much as the water. Her hands were clutching the rail like nothing and no one could pry them free.

She was right. He wasn't feeling the heat, either. Not like last night.

Making love, he had wanted to give her more, give her everything. Physically, they had never been closer. And yet now, he was up against that wall of hers again.

He rested his hand next to hers on the rail. "What have we got planned for today?"

"I'm going to relax," she said, closing her eyes and tipping her face more toward the warmth of the sun.

"Relaxing sounds good."

She took in a deep breath but kept her eyes shut. "What are you going to do? I guess you need to get back. Work to do."

He took in a group of guests relaxing on sun loungers on the beach. "I'll stay on. Hang out."

When she finally opened her eyes and slid him a look, he moved to cover her hand with his. But she was already turning away, heading back inside. He frowned at his bare feet for a moment, weighing things up. Did she want him to simply say, *Thanks for the sex, see ya later,* and walk away? That would make her evaluation of him right, but it was an empty victory if you asked him.

Inside, he found her flicking through some hotel literature. Hitching up his shoulders, he shoved both hands in his pockets and got the words out.

"I meant what I said last night, Veda. The last thing I want to do is hurt you."

The brochure crinkled as her grip tightened. Then she shook her head slightly. "Doesn't matter."

"It matters."

Her eyes met his. "Don't you want to know why I was suddenly falling all over you yesterday?"

Well, yeah. "I was curious."

"I was testing a theory. The one that goes, 'girl full-on chases Ajax. Ajax gets bored and gets another girl.' It didn't take long."

"Veda, that woman and I were just talking. I wasn't bored."

She crossed her arms. "Really?"

He hesitated.

"Look, I've had more exciting evenings," he admitted, "but that had absolutely nothing to do with you." And about that theory… "You decided to throw yourself at me so I'd get bored? Why?"

"To speed up the inevitable. To prove the theory right. Just look at your track record. You *must* be all about the challenge."

He crossed over to her, took her hands and held on. "I came here to be with you. No one else."

"For however long that lasts."

"Well… Yeah. That's right."

Her eyebrows shot up. "At least you're admitting it now."

"Yesterday, after our drink at the bar," he explained, "I felt on edge. If we ended up in bed again, I wasn't sure how it would be the next day between us. I wasn't sure how I would feel come morning. Not because I was bored, Veda." He put it out there. "Because I haven't felt like this about anyone before."

She blinked several times, then pressed her lips together.

"That's another line," she said.

He smiled into her eyes. "Let's just go with the flow. See where this takes us."

"You mean despite my father despising your family, and Hux probably thinking I'm some kind of spy?"

"Don't forget the fact that you hate the profession that I love."

"And neither of us wants anything serious."

That got him. *Serious* was an interesting word.

And best not think about that now because he could see that he might have turned this ship around.

Her lips almost twitched. "So, what's your idea of going with the flow while we're here?"

Squeezing her hands, he winked.

"Put on your swimsuit," he said, "and I'll show you."

"Here's something you don't know about me," Ajax said, while they settled into a pair of sun lounges set up in a quiet nook of the extensive pool area. "It's my biggest secret. You'll never guess."

As Veda heeled off her sandals, she slid him a look. Now this could be interesting. Ajax was pretty straightforward. Openly charming. Explicitly sexy. Here for a good time, not a long time. Whether he was actually flirting with that woman last night wasn't the point. His history of short-but-sweet was the problem.

And yet when he had knocked on her door, Veda had looked into those dreamy blue eyes and rolled over. Which could be viewed as weak or simply taking what she wanted. And, of course, she hadn't been disappointed. Ajax had a way of bringing out the very best in her, with his hands and his tongue and his...well, *everything*. This morning, however, she'd been torn between wanting to jump on him again and wondering whether he was thinking she was way too easy.

And that's how she had ended up here, making the decision to simply relax in the Barbados sunshine with Ajax and his drool-worthy body. This man was her Achilles' heel, and ultimately, there would be a price to pay. But not today.

Not today.

He was talking about his biggest secret...

"Let's see." Pretending to think long and hard, she tapped her chin. "You love soppy movies?"

"Other than *The Longest Ride*, not a chance."

"You're an alien conspiracy diehard."

"Really good guess, but no tamale."

"You think only one game of football should be televised per week."

He chuckled. "My secret is that I used to be afraid of water. Couldn't swim. Not a stroke."

Veda slid her gaze from him to the pool, then back again. "You did say used to be, right? How'd you get over it?"

"Hux had the same fear when he was a kid," he said, flipping the lid open on the sunscreen. "Want me to do your shoulders?"

After ditching her wrap, she swept her hair to one side. Her swimsuit wasn't anything outrageously sexy—just a semi-fitted white tankini top that fell to her navel and black bikini bottoms that pretty much covered both cheeks.

"Is Griff afraid of water, too?" she asked, turning around. "I haven't heard Lanie ever mention it."

"Just me and Dad," he said as a big, hot, border-line rough hand smeared cream between her shoulder blades. "We have a huge pool at home. One summer when I was eight, he had me in there every day. It took a while but he was patient."

Veda's eyes drifted shut. He was using both hands now, working over her shoulders and down her arms.

Feeling a little dreamy, she asked, "So you went on to win every race at the school meets?"

"I never won a ribbon in the pool." He was close behind her now, reaching around to rub her thighs. "But I no longer freak out at the thought of my head going under, so all good." He made a shivering sound. "I'll never forget the feeling, though. Total panic."

"I can identify."

"You needed heavy-duty swimming lessons, too?"

"Heavy-duty *reading* lessons." She took a breath and let it all out. "I'm dyslexic." When she felt his hands draw away, she turned back around. "I get letters confused," she said. "Jumbled. Back to front."

"Dyslexic. Right." He nodded, then nodded again. "I mean, I've heard of it."

"It set me back when I was younger, in a whole lot of ways."

"You mean at school?"

"I didn't understand why other kids weren't turned off by books or writing the way I was. I didn't get how they put letters together to make words, let alone sentences. I actually thought it was some kind of joke and I was the punch line."

"So when did the teacher tell your parents?"

"I wasn't diagnosed until years later."

He rocked back. "You mean you went all the way through struggling like that?"

The sunscreen bottle lay on the lounger next to his leg. She grabbed it up and explained, "I did really well in math. Maybe it's a compensatory thing, but my brain does way better with numbers."

"Getting through something like that... It must be a huge inspiration for the people you coach."

She held off squirting sunscreen into her palm. "We were talking about secrets, remember?"

"Oh. So who else knows?"

"My dad. Now you. Turn around."

He swung his legs over to the lounger's other side and then there was his back...bare, broad and perfectly bronzed. As she rubbed the hot, smooth slopes on either side of his neck, she imagined him working in the sun with his horses, sans shirt, jeans riding low.

"So you're obviously over it," he said as she continued to stroke and rub.

"You don't get over dyslexia. But you can learn to work with it. In a lot of ways, I don't think of it as a disability. I had to try harder at a lot of things. Some of my grades sucked. But along the way I've learned other stuff like keeping things clear-cut and how to delegate. I've honed my concentration skills and try to listen to intuition."

His beautiful shoulders rolled back. "How did your parents react when they found out?"

Her stomach balled up before she squeezed more sunscreen into her palm. "It was after my mom died."

He paused before asking, "Did your dad help?"

"Not like yours with the swimming." Her father hadn't been hands-on. "He took me to professionals." For her dyslexia and also to help manage her grief. "He's never been big on communication." She rubbed Ajax's back again, painting a big circle, then sweeping her hand up and down. "Maybe that's where I get it from." Maybe Drake was dyslexic, too. Sure, she saw him with books, reading. That didn't mean it was easy.

"Veda, you're a great communicator. I was glued to my seat listening to you on that stage yesterday."

"Ha! You were not."

He turned back around. "No lie."

"Well, I'm not a natural at it. The big D held me back in a lot of ways other than schoolwork. I was socially awkward through the roof. I never felt like I fit. Some kids at school made it way worse."

"You were bullied."

She nodded. "Whenever I got stressed, like if I had to read in front of class, my brain would freeze. It literally wouldn't work. I'd get this feeling like fingers closing around my throat. No words would come out. I was completely mute."

He leaned closer. "When was the last time it happened?"

"Not for ages. Until a little attack at Lanie's party when she introduced me to your dad and then left us alone."

"But Dad's easy to talk to."

"He is. But remember our family feud? Huge trigger. I got a few words out but by the time he left, Hux thought I was a kook. That's the other thing. When you have this problem, which is *not* the same as being shy, people don't know what to make of it. Make of you. Some wonder if you're just too stuck-up to talk to them, or maybe your IQ must be low." She winced. "Really not a nice place to be."

When he took her hand and smiled, her everything, inside and out, smiled, too.

"This is what we're going to do," he said. "We're going to swim out into the middle of that pool. I'm going to keep us afloat and listen while you tell me all about what's next on the Veda Darnel Kick Ass agenda."

Still smiling, she nodded. "I like that idea."

Hand in hand, they waded in and then freestyled out until the water was up to his chest and she couldn't touch the bottom. Then he wrapped his arms around her waist and twirled.

"Not feeling anxious?" she asked, holding on to his shoulders and winding her legs around his hips.

"Not in the least. Feeling good. Feeling *great*. And I'm listening."

"Well, if you really want to know, large scale, I do have a dream. I don't know when but I feel it'll happen sometime, even if it's when I need dentures and three naps a day. I would love to have a quiet acre or two for a rescue farm," she said.

"What kind of animals? Because I can't possibly guess."

"Right. Horses. But also sheep, chickens, ducks,

pigs. Actually, did you know pigs are supposed to be more intelligent than dogs?"

A sexy grin hooked his mouth. "I did not know that."

"Some say pigs are the fifth most intelligent animal in the world. They're capable of learning how to do simple jigsaw puzzles and work basic remote controls."

"*Sold.* We definitely need lots of pigs."

She laughed at his gorgeous smiling eyes. "Lots of everything."

"You might need more than a couple acres then."

"Sure. Like I said. It's a ways off yet."

His hands were sliding up and down her back, making her tingle…making her hot.

"So, what are you going to call your first pet pig?"

"Well, Wilbur and Babe are already taken."

"Porky, too." Sliding and swirling, he touched his nose to hers. "I've got one for a sheep. Baa-bardos."

She smothered a bigger smile. "And people say you aren't funny."

"Oh, yeah? Want to hear a dirty joke?"

"Do I have a choice?"

"A white horse fell in a puddle of mud."

Before she could roll her eyes, he started tickling her ribs until she was splashing around, laughing so hard.

"I can do this all day," he said. "Take it back. Take it back."

"Okay, okay! You're funny. *So* funny."

"And you're beautiful. And really easy to tickle." He came in to graze his lips over hers. His deep voice rumbled through her when he said, "I'm glad we're here together."

Catching her breath, easing out a sigh, she ran her palms over his warm, wet shoulders. "I'm glad we are, too."

As he held her by the hips, his eyes drifted shut. Then he nipped her lower lip and ran the tip of his tongue over the seam.

"What's your intuition saying now?" he murmured, staying close.

"That you need to prove just how good you are in the water."

When she found his arousal well below the surface, his mouth automatically claimed hers. By the time he broke the kiss, in Veda's mind, they were completely alone. In their own world.

She shivered as he nibbled that sensitive sweep of her neck.

"Veda?" he asked.

Eyes closed, she cupped his scratchy jaw. "Hmm?"

"I think we need to go back to the room."

And then he was kissing her again, and in that wet, steamy, crazy-for-you moment, she was already thinking about next time…dreaming about seeing her Ajax again.

Ten

Early the next morning, Veda and Ajax said a reluctant goodbye at the airport before boarding separate flights. Back in New Jersey hours later, still unpacking while smiling over the memories, Veda answered a knock on her condo door and almost fell over. This was the last person she expected to show up unannounced today. And, given her ongoing fling with Ajax, pretty much the last person she wanted to see.

"I was down this way," her father said, placing his tweed duckbill cap on the hatstand as he made a point of stepping around her to walk inside.

She took a moment to remember to breathe while Drake assessed the surroundings, taking a token interest in the bookshelf while running a fingertip over the self-help titles. He had asked for her address ages ago but had never arranged to visit, let alone simply dropped in.

"Well…can I get you something to drink?" she asked.

"Green tea?" He retrieved a handkerchief from his dress pants pocket and wiped his fingertip clean. "Very hot."

"I have coffee. Freshly brewed."

He took a moment to accept that option and then added, "No sugar, of course."

Walking to the kitchen, she felt rather than heard him behind her. For as long as she could remember, Drake had worn the same aftershave. More often than not, the scent stirred feelings of unease. As she had told Ajax yesterday, Drake wasn't a total monster; after her mother's accident, he had gotten her help. But he wasn't demonstrative as far as fatherly affection was concerned. He certainly hadn't shown love toward his wife.

Now the nostrils of his long thin nose flared like he was either opposed to the aroma of her coffee or, more likely, the space in general. Her condo was the polar opposite of Darnel Manor, as in modern and personal rather than ridiculously grand and, in so many ways, stuck in the past.

"There's a courtyard," she said, retrieving cups from the cabinet. "It's such a nice day out."

He nodded, then asked, "How long have you been here now?"

"Three years. It's home."

He grunted—the sound someone might make when they were on the verge of being bored stiff.

She led him through to the courtyard, which was littered with fallen leaves and petals from a vine. As she set down their cups on the tabletop, Drake snapped out his handkerchief again to dust down his seat.

"Are you staying in the city?" she asked, taking a chair. Drake had friends in Manhattan.

"I'm here to speak with you."

Veda caught something knowing lurking in the shadows of his eyes and then, of course, this shock visit made sense. Drake must have heard through the grapevine that she was romantically involved with a Rawson and couldn't wait to express his opinion. On the outside, he was his usual uptight self. On the inside—oh, how it must bite.

His question, "Is it true?" confirmed her guess.

She wasn't after a fight. Nor would she lie or shrivel up in a corner.

"Yes." She lifted her cup. "It's true."

He carefully lowered himself into his chair. "You're asking for trouble. You know that, don't you? It was bad enough when you became friends with the girl."

"You mean Lanie Rawson."

"Yes. *Rawson*." His lips pursed and twitched. "I can't believe it. Can't believe it of my own daughter. You know the kind of people they are. The kind of *men*. The father has no scruples. And the sons…" He made a face like bile had risen in his throat. "I wouldn't be the least surprised if they all had diseases."

"Like Ebola?"

"Sexually transmitted."

After tsking, he took a mouthful of coffee, rather inelegantly, Veda thought.

"That boy is even worse than his father," he said.

"Worse?" She arched a brow. "Or better?"

Drake's chin began to quiver. Not because he was going to cry. Because he was livid and showing it.

"I didn't think you could ever betray me like this. Not like this."

Using that grudge from his past as an excuse to act out had been warped enough when he'd used it against her mother.

"You do realize that I'm your daughter, right? Not the woman who left you for Hux Rawson."

Getting to his feet, he retrieved something from his shirt pocket—a page torn from a magazine—and read it out loud.

"'Ajax Rawson, also known as the Stud, was spotted with another beautiful female companion. Life coach Veda Darnel, daughter of longtime Rawsons critic Drake Darnel, looks smitten. We wish her luck.'"

Her father was coming around the table, standing beside her, almost begging.

"Veda…darling…he'll hurt you. Then he'll leave you."

She glared at him. "Because everyone leaves you, Dad?"

She and Drake had words after that. She said some things that she'd kept buried for way too long. And she was still pacing, fuming, long after he'd left.

She didn't owe that man an explanation. This was

her life now, not her mother's and certainly not his. And yet in some ways she felt fourteen again, when her father could barely look at her because she had sided with her mom. Now she wondered more than ever: Would Drake have loved her less or more if he ever found out she was responsible for the death of his wife?

When her cell phone rang later that day, Veda had almost succeeded in pushing her father out of her mind. She needed positivity in her life, not smothering and controlling.

When she answered the call, an official-sounding woman asked to confirm with whom she was speaking. Then this woman passed on all the information that she had…said she was sorry…and, yes, most definitely… it would be wise to come to the hospital right away.

When Ajax arrived back at the farm, all kinds of shit was hitting the fan.

Even before entering the office building, he heard the raised voice. Striding through, he found his private door open. When he saw papers and files strewn all over the damn place, he was so taken aback, he couldn't contain the growl.

"What the hell is going on?"

Hux sat behind Ajax's desk, poring over an assortment of splayed documents. When he looked up from the mess, his eyes were more unhinged than blue.

"What do you *think* is going on?" Hux fell back in the high-backed chair. "Did you even bother to open Jacob's messages?"

Charging forward, Ajax started stacking papers. "I spoke to Jacob an hour ago."

"So you know they want to look through your veterinary records."

"We went over them two weeks ago. There's nothing to see."

"The stewards have scheduled a meeting with you and Booshang this Friday. After the delay, the test results are expected to land that morning."

"We'll be ready. If there's a fine or suspension, we'll deal with it."

Hux shot to his feet. "Damn it, Ajax! This is serious."

For God's sake. "My books and stables are *clean.*"

"A Triple Crown trainer...and now your reputation will be—"

"Hux, get off my back!"

His father's eyes blazed before he moved to the window to gaze out over the stables. "Yesterday, two clients loaded their horses and took them away."

Which clients? What horses?

Exhaling, Ajax shoved the documents aside. "They'll come back when this is sorted out."

"And if there's a next time?"

Ajax studied his father and said it out loud.

"You can't seriously think I'm actually involved in this."

Hux slumped and shook his head. "No, no. Of course not."

"Then what were you thinking going through all this? There's nothing to find here. I told you. I'm clean…even if a lot of other trainers can't say the same."

Hux waved that away, but it was a valid point. As much as he loved horse racing, Veda was right. Everyone in the industry knew that doping, or at the very least overmedicating, was a problem.

Hux visibly gathered himself before asking, "Where were you this weekend?"

"I haven't had a day off in months. I needed a break."

"With the Darnel girl?"

"Her name is Veda." He grabbed his work hat, stuck it on his head. "And she's not a girl."

"Don't you think it's strange that she suddenly befriended Lanie and now you? When we spoke alone at the party, frankly I thought she was hiding something."

"Like she'd joined her father and Booshang in a vendetta against us?" *Oh, please.* Ajax headed for the door. "We don't know that Drake is involved in any way."

"Griff heard his name mentioned that night. Darnel is spouting off to the press."

Ajax had his doubts, too, but, "That's not proof. And it's certainly not any reason to ransack my office and send the hounds after Veda."

While Ajax stood at the door, his demeanor more than implying that Hux needed to leave, Hux's expression changed from frustration to something akin to enlightenment. His voice was a disbelieving rasp.

"My God. Ajax…you're serious about her, aren't you?"

"Dad, that's none of your business."

"You've always wanted to do things your own way,"

Hux said, moving closer. "Always wanted to lead the pack. Make an impression."

"If you mean like working my ass off to keep this place afloat when you could barely drag yourself out of bed—" Ajax thumped the door "—yeah, I lead the pack."

"Your mother had died—" Hux snapped his fingers "—just like that."

"She'd been sick for months." Ajax swallowed hard. "And she was my mother as much as your wife. Damn it, I was hurting, too. But I kept pushing forward." He gritted his teeth, shook his head and ground the words out. "I never understood why you resented that."

"I'm sure I've thanked you, and way more than once."

"With a clap on the back and a wage that hardly reflects what I bring in for this place. Griff just has to smile and you gush over how brilliant he is. I'll puke if I have to hear again how proud you are of Jacob."

Hux pulled a pained face. "You're jealous of your brothers?"

"I'm tired of bending over backward trying to please you." Ajax squared his shoulders. "This place would fall apart without me."

Hux's chin lifted. "Please don't think you're indispensable, because, I can assure you, none of us are."

When his father stormed out, Ajax fought the urge to follow and bawl him out some more. It hurt like hell to have that conversation. Hux was a good father, but this had been brewing for too long. Since his mother had passed away, rather than a son, Ajax had felt like an employee needing to jump through higher and higher hoops. Well, he was sick and tired of proving himself.

He slammed the door and wandered over to the window. An assistant trainer was working with a new boarder in the arena. In the lower paddock, a stallion was shaking his mane, enjoying the sunshine. Ajax loved this life, from keeping a close eye on foaling rates to writing up owner updates and finalizing racing nominations.

But what was his future here? He wanted his father to live to a hundred, but was he prepared to do pretty much all of the work only to be reminded in times like these that he wasn't really in charge? Had Hux ever truly considered handing over the reins one day?

And Veda...

No one would tell him whom he could or could not see. And if his father didn't like it—if Hux had suspicions with regard to Veda's motives—he could blow it out his pipe. Because Veda was not working with her father to bring them all down. She had way more integrity than that. He'd bet his life on it.

Ajax drew out his phone.

He might come across sounding needy, but he had to hear her voice about now. Although it had started off shaky, their time in Barbados has been the best. They had parted with an understanding that they would see each other again soon, and he appreciated that was a huge deal for her.

It was for him, too.

"Ajax?"

The boost he felt from hearing her say his name

didn't last long. Rather than sounding pleased that he'd called, in that single word she sounded upset. Panicked even. He pressed the phone closer to his ear.

"Veda, are you okay?"

Obviously on speaker, she talked in a series of halting phrases. There'd been another phone call. She had left immediately. Would be there inside half an hour.

"Whoa. Hold on. You're driving up here? I'm guessing this has something to do with your dad."

"There's been an accident," she said, followed by a sharp intake of breath. "He's in the hospital."

Ajax's priorities did a one-eighty.

"Which hospital?" He was already rushing for the door, car remote in hand. "Don't worry, honey. I'll meet you there."

Eleven

Veda had kept it together the entire drive from Jersey, but when she saw Ajax waiting for her as she ran from her parked car to the hospital's entrance, all that built-up emotion threatened to break through. Being told that her father had been in a serious car accident had thrown her like nothing else could. Now she flung herself into Ajax's open arms and dissolved as he stroked her hair and murmured her name.

"It's okay, Veda. We'll go in together. I'm sure he'll be fine."

She dashed away tears she'd held back until now. "Apparently he was only a few minutes from home when he ran off the road. He said he thought he saw something…"

"So he's conscious?"

She nodded as they headed inside. "He hit a tree."

Walking to the elevator, Ajax held her hand so tight, it almost hurt. But she only gripped his hand back in return. God, how she needed an anchor...this depth of support.

Earlier on the phone, the administrator had passed on ward details. At the nurses' station, Veda provided her father's name, approximate time of arrival and reason for admittance. When the nurse looked up from the computer screen after checking, Veda knew something more was wrong.

The nurse adjusted her eyeglasses and tried on a smile as she got to her feet. "I'll see if I can find a doctor. Please, take a seat."

Veda's face began to tingle and go warm. As she turned to Ajax, the room seemed to slope and wobble on its axis. This wasn't the hospital her mom had been rushed to after that other accident, but it looked the same, smelled the same, and the look on that nurse's face...

Veda was aware of Ajax's hands bracing her upper arms as he rushed to reassure her. The nurse wouldn't be long. He was sure that Drake was all right. The entire drive here, Veda had told herself that same thing: as big a shock as this was, her father would be fine. But her thoughts were bombarded with phrases like *Fate can be cruel* and *History might not repeat itself but it often rhymes*. She seemed to have always been at war with Drake, but that didn't mean she wanted him taken from her, particularly the same way she had lost her mom.

A tall man with a lilting voice was introducing himself...the name badge said Dr. Wasley...or was that Sawley?

Veda couldn't wait a second longer. She had to know.

"Is he dead?"

The doctor's onyx eyes smiled as he reassured her. "Your father is very much alive. Apparently a deer leaped out and collided with his vehicle. No fractures, although we want to keep an eye on a minor head injury. A graze and bump on his head. He's a lucky man to have gotten off so lightly."

Ajax asked, "When can Veda see him?"

The doctor's mouth pressed into a harder line before he replied. "Ms. Darnel, your father has asked that he not be disturbed at this time."

Veda blinked, shook her head. "But does he know that I'm here?"

"He gave your name as next of kin." The doctor paused. "But I'm afraid he doesn't want visitors."

Veda was ready to ask that someone look into that again. But then the nurse's expression a moment ago began to make sense. She'd been reacting to the situation of a daughter rushing to an injured father who didn't want to see her. It was sad. Awkward.

The doctor tried to rationalize. "Oftentimes, people are embarrassed at having lost control of a vehicle. They might need time to overcome feelings of having let others down, as they perceive it." He offered a reassuring smile. "I'm certain he'll come around."

As the doctor left, Ajax looped his arms around her

and Veda leaned in. He felt real when, at this moment, nothing else did.

"We'll hang around," Ajax said, stroking her arm as she nestled against him. "You can be here when he comes to his senses."

"And if that doesn't happen?"

"Like the doctor said…he's got issues with having screwed up."

"So he shuts me out. Typical." She stepped back. "Well, I'm not going to give him the satisfaction of being pathetic enough to wait."

Ajax's gaze softened further. "Maybe just a few minutes. He knows you're here. Let that sink in. He's obviously not thinking straight."

"He's thinking like he always does. About himself."

After their argument this morning, had Drake purposely wrecked his car for a sympathy vote? To snap his recalcitrant daughter back into line? Hell, she'd dropped everything to race here, hadn't she?

"Sorry," she told Ajax, heading off. "I've got to go."

"You can't drive back to Jersey," he said, catching up. "You shouldn't be driving anywhere right now. Your father might be acting like a dick, but you're smarter than that."

Stabbing the elevator call button, she tried to settle her emotions.

"You're right. I'll take a cab. Go back to Dad's place…catch my breath."

"I'll drive. And sit with you for a while."

She darted him a look. "You mean actually come into enemy territory?"

The corners of his mouth twitched. "Boy, wouldn't that piss him off."

Veda hesitated. Then she smiled. Finally she laughed because, hell, what else could she do.

As the elevator doors slid open, she linked her arm through Ajax's and, after this crazy, stress-filled morning, announced to the world, "Let's really tick Drake off. My God, let's make him howl!"

Veda had gotten her spark back before they'd left the hospital, but she'd gone quiet while he'd driven her car back to Darnel Manor. Obviously she was still dwelling on the accident, as well as Drake's latest dick move. He had manipulated a highly emotionally charged situation by refusing to see, and comfort, his own daughter.

Ajax didn't buy into the doctor's explanation about her father feeling embarrassed over totaling his car. Something major was up between father and daughter, and Ajax had the feeling it centered on him.

Passing through the open Darnel gates, he took note of the endless stream of soaring pines lining the drive. At the top of the first hill stood a massive stone-and-shingle structure that captured the essence of an over-the-top bygone era. After parking the SUV out front, he escorted Veda to the colossal cherrywood double entry doors. Looking around, Ajax couldn't make out any sign of the stables, arenas, paddocks—no horses or people were anywhere to be seen.

Then they stepped inside and Ajax almost lost his breakfast.

This place was the Gilded Age on steroids. The

foyer was three stories of imported marble, gold trimmings and hardwood parquet flooring and had enough classical sculptures to man a football team.

He realized Veda was studying him and snapped his hanging jaw shut. "A wood shack this is not."

She hugged herself as if battling a chill. "It feels like a huge, creepy mausoleum, right?"

"I wasn't going to say that." *Out loud.*

"Mom never felt comfortable here. But that wasn't totally the house's fault."

"Must take an army of people to keep up appearances," he said, blowing imaginary dust off a Greek goddess's head.

"My father gets someone in three times a year to give everything a resounding polish. Other than that, I can't tell you whether anyone walks through those front doors anymore. Aside from me on occasion. And, I guess, someone to drop off groceries."

So Drake didn't allow his trainers, grooms, riders, farriers and other employees to enter his sanctuary. He preferred to conduct business at the stable office. A little Howard Hughes, but sure. Okay.

"Doesn't he at least have a cook?"

"Far too intrusive," she said with a manufactured air. "And he is the world's best chef. Just ask him." She cocked her head. "Ajax, are you hungry?"

Come to think of it. "I could squeeze in a little something."

She led him into a kitchen that continued the lavish theme, with an exclamation point. Compared to

Susan's kitchen, this room looked so *big*. And lonely. The word *haunted* also came to mind.

Veda opened the refrigerator door and cobbled together ingredients for sandwiches. While he slapped mayo on the bread and she cut lettuce, tomato and cheese, he tried to picture her growing up in this place. He felt ill just thinking about it. But the stark formality fit with everything he knew about Drake Darnel, including his rebuff of Veda today.

He thought he was pretty darn special.

"I never felt like this was a home," she said, laying fillings on the bread. "I don't know how my mother suffered it for so long."

"What was the tipping point?"

"In the marriage? Drake accused her of having an affair with one of the stable hands. My father isn't much of a conversationalist at the best of times. After that, it was the silent treatment every night." Veda sliced the sandwiches, and while Ajax put them onto a plate, she found a chilled bottle of juice. "I challenge anyone to live in this kind of environment for any length of time," she said, leading the way through a door that connected with a colossal-sized sun room. "Slowly but surely, let me tell you, it drains the soul."

The hexagonal room was surrounded by soaring floor-to-ceiling French windows. Ajax could admit that the view of the hills was pretty—similar, of course, to a view from his home.

They sat together on an ornate red velvet couch and dug in while looking out over the vista. On his second bite, Ajax's phone rang. After checking the ID, he put the phone away.

"You can take it," Veda said. "Don't mind me."

"It was Hux."

"You didn't want to lie about where you were?"

"I don't give a crap whether he knows or not."

She lowered her sandwich. "That doesn't sound good."

Recalling their argument earlier that day was almost enough to put him off his food. "I love that man. He's a great father and mentor. But sometimes...he just doesn't get it."

"This is about that doping allegation."

"Yes. And no."

Ajax explained how he'd gotten home that morning to find Hux riffling through his office files, and then shared the news that a meeting regarding those allegations was scheduled for the end of the week, *and* some clients had decided to take their horses elsewhere.

"Hux and I have never had an argument like that before, and I'm over it. I love what I do, but sometimes, like today... He doesn't know how much I give."

Veda looked taken aback. "Sorry. I thought everything was hunky-dory in the Rawson camp."

"Ask the others and they'd agree. Griff, Lanie, Jacob...he supports and encourages them without a second thought. But me? I feel like I have to earn his approval every day."

"Have you always felt that way?"

"Since Mom passed. You know about me putting that ad up and finding Susan."

"That was so brave."

Ajax didn't see it as courageous but simply as necessity. "Everyone was so down. Someone had to get things moving again. I had to at least try to make people smile and forget." He flinched. "I sound like I'm whining, don't I?"

"No. Not at all." She smiled softly. "Ajax, you found a way to save your family. I think that is the noblest thing anyone can do."

His throat was suddenly thick. No one would ever know, and he would never forget, how desperate he'd felt at the time. He had wanted to save his family. What was left of it, at least.

"I felt so stifled living under my dad's say-so," Veda said, and then clarified, "I know Hux isn't anything like my father... Just saying."

"When did you leave?"

"Freshman year of college. Never looked back."

"I didn't do college. Too much to do at home."

"Did you want to go?"

"When I was young, I wanted to be a vet."

"Well, there you go!"

"That was a long time ago."

"Hey, there's nothing wrong with starting a little late." She thought a moment before squeezing his arm then getting to her feet. "I'd like to show you something. I mean if you're not in a hurry to get back or anything."

Ready to shake all the bad feelings out, he jumped up. "Veda, I'm all yours."

* * *

Seeing the tree house again brought back a flood of memories and emotions. Perched in a rambling old oak ten feet above the ground, the timber hideaway was the size of a modest bedroom and had once been home to Veda's favorite dolls and games. Here she had felt totally happy. Truly safe.

"I had a little dog growing up," Veda said as she and Ajax drew closer to the tree house. "Gus was my best friend. I used to climb up this ladder and he'd jump in that." She crossed over to a faded blue plastic bucket with a hairy old rope tied to its handle. "Then I'd pull him up."

"Gus… I'm thinking a beagle."

"A cream teacup poodle. He had apricot smudges on his cheeks like an old lady had done his makeup. Dad brought him home for me on my fifth birthday. I even caught Gus snuggled up on Drake's lap a few times."

Looking up at the tree house, Ajax grabbed a ladder rung. It snapped, rotten all the way through.

He winced. "I'll fix it for you."

"Don't worry. This must be fifty or sixty years old. An employee from the stables used to patch it up for me."

"Sounds like you had a friend."

She arched a brow. "It was Paul Booshang."

His head kicked back. "Get outta here."

"And he *was* a friend. Mom's, too. I don't think he liked the way Drake ignored my mother and me."

"I don't suppose you knew anything about him doping horses back then."

She shook her head. "And neither did my father, or Paul would've found a boot up his backside. In case you haven't noticed, my father is not a tolerant man, even where family is concerned. I'm sure Paul wasn't the only staff member to feel sorry for me and Mom. It got worse after she said we would leave if things didn't change. Once it got so heated, he slapped her."

She kicked the bucket and the old plastic split into brittle pieces at the same time Ajax drew up to his full intimidating height.

"Did he ever touch you?"

"Never. In fact, the night we packed up to leave, he asked me to stay." Remembering how torn she had felt…how lost… Veda shuddered. "Believe it or not, I cried walking out the door."

Ajax stepped closer. "I'm sorry you had such a hard time growing up. It must seem like a long time ago now."

Actually, it didn't feel that long ago at all.

"Dad came by to see me earlier," she said.

"You mean in New Jersey? Today?"

"We argued. And yes, it was about us."

He blinked as he put it together. "Veda, if you feel guilty over your father's accident because he might've been upset—"

"I don't feel guilty." She fought down a shiver. "I absolutely don't."

Anyway, that was enough about Drake. Enough about the past.

"When I stay over now, I use the guesthouse." She nodded toward the beautiful old stone building. "It was here before the main house was built."

Following her gaze, Ajax's eyebrows shot up. "The Rawson original has a long way to go before it looks anywhere near as good as that." He brought out his phone and pulled up a few photos.

"Oh, it's sweet," she said, taking in the Cape Cod with its steep pitched roof and big front door centered below a massive chimney.

"I should show you around sometime," he said, slotting the phone away.

"My turn first," she said, grabbing his hand and heading toward the guesthouse.

"We'll need keys."

"Got them in my pocket."

He grinned. "I like how you think."

"I like how you feel…" Turning back and into his arms, she nuzzled his warm, salty neck. "How you taste."

When he kissed her, Veda felt her world shift that much more toward a new way of thinking and feeling. Once she had been happiest here alone, just her and little Gus. Now she was happiest when she was with Ajax. Right now, she felt safe.

Maybe even loved.

Twelve

When Ajax drove his truck up to the house early the next morning, an unfamiliar vehicle was parked in the guest area.

If Hux had company, Ajax was happy to take a coffee on the back porch and wait until his father was free. He'd been mad as hell after their argument. Since talking it through and spending the night with Veda, however, he had calmed down.

Not that his opinion had changed on anything, Ajax thought, taking the front steps two at a time. He hated the doping allegation hanging over his head. He was sorry that some clients had opted out. But he wasn't unhappy that this episode had brought to the fore his growing concerns regarding his standing here at Rawson's. He had felt like the hired help for too long.

So now it was crunch time, Ajax reaffirmed as he headed for the kitchen and the coffeepot. He and Hux would have a conversation today highlighting the fact that fair was fair. He wanted a partnership agreement drawn up by the end of the week or he would need to consider his other options.

When he pushed through the swing doors, he found Susan standing by the center counter. Her eyes widened before her usual welcoming smile took over.

"Ajax. What good timing."

That's when he noticed their company. Five foot one. A hundred and ten pounds. Thick shoulder-length blond hair that she usually wore in a ponytail but was loose today. He was used to seeing her in training gear or jockey silks, not a dress. But her smile was the same. Big. Contagious.

He headed over and gave their guest a big, warm hug. She didn't smell a bit like leather and horse sweat. In fact, her scent brought to mind a summer garden.

"Fallon Kelly." Pulling back, he took his friend in again. "This is a surprise."

Fallon's chocolate-brown eyes were dancing. "I was driving through on my way to Vermont. I hoped y'all wouldn't mind if I dropped in."

Susan set a cup of coffee on the counter beside Ajax. "She looks well, doesn't she?"

"She looks *amazing*," Ajax replied.

Susan was headed for the swing doors. "You two get caught up while I tell Huxley you're here, Fallon. And I'll let him know you're home, Jax."

Susan and Hux didn't have secrets; she would know

all about yesterday's blowup. Not that she ever inserted herself into family matters, which was nuts given she *was* family.

Ajax led Fallon out back and they took seats that offered a magic view of the hills. Dew was still glistening on everything green. The sky was a dome of early heaven-sent blue. If he squinted, he could even see the roof of the original house from here.

"It must be a year since we saw you last," he said. "Just after you gave up riding."

"Doesn't seem that long ago."

He thought about his own situation—about weighing up his choices—and asked, "Do you miss the racing scene?"

"I miss the special bond I have with a horse. I don't miss those early mornings and worrying about every little thing I put in my mouth."

Ajax hooked an arm over the back of the bench as he turned more toward her. "I'll never forget our big win at Belmont Park."

"I had a great ride. Kudos to the wonderful trainer." She tipped toward him, grinning.

And then, for just a second, her gaze dropped from his eyes to his lips, which prompted a whole other line of recollection. After that win and celebratory drinks, he and Fallon had gotten together—a single night that hadn't developed into anything more. Her career was her main focus. Or so he had thought. He'd been blindsided when she'd said that she wanted to pursue other goals.

"So what are you up to now?" he asked.

"I've been in Kentucky with family, thinking about

starting a riding school. Nothing snooty. I'm more interested in being laid-back. In having fun."

Sounded good compared to the ruckus going on around here of late.

"What's been happening in your life, Jax?" she asked, before taking a long sip from her steaming cup.

"I'm surprised you haven't heard the rumblings, even all the way down in Louisville."

"You mean the rumor that you're into doping now?"

His grin was entirely humorless. "So, you *have* heard."

"I want you to know that I support you one hundred percent. And what the hell is with Paul Booshang anyway? I'd always thought he was a good guy. Trying to fix a race is bad enough. Dragging you into it is unbelievable." She took another sip and then asked, "Do you think Booshang is a lone wolf, hoping he could make a sure bet on the side, or is he in cahoots with someone else?"

"I'm not sure I should go into that."

Fallon's eyes rounded. "So there *is* someone else."

"Nothing's been proven. Not by a long shot." When she arched a brow, he grunted and gave it up. "We've heard Drake Darnel's name mentioned."

But after hearing Veda's tree house story, it didn't sound as if Booshang had ever been a fan of Drake's. So why would Paul work covertly with him now?

"Darnel Stables has an impeccable reputation. But as far as the man himself is concerned…" She visibly shuddered. "Do you know, after our win in Elmont, he flat-out scowled at me."

"His filly finished second."

"Drake Darnel is a stinking bad loser." She shrugged. "Still, I can't see him shooting his horses up. He's too darn self-righteous. But he does hate your dad. He'd tell anyone who listened that good training was not the reason your horses won."

"Meaning we had to be using performance enhancing drugs."

"I guess no one's surprised that his daughter thinks the same."

Ajax sat up. "Veda?"

"Uh-huh." Fallon sipped her coffee. "That's her name."

"So, you've heard that with your own ears? Veda saying that we break the law? Cheat?"

Fallon looked taken aback. "I've never spoken to her personally. But I think it's common knowledge what she thought of the industry."

Susan appeared at the door.

"Huxley is on a conference call," she told them. "He'll be a while. But I've pulled a batch of blueberry muffins out of the oven if anyone's interested."

Fallon smacked her lips. "I can smell them from here. Can you put one away for me?" she asked, getting to her feet. "I was hoping Ajax might take me on a tour of the stables while the sun's not too high in the sky."

"I'll let Huxley know where you're at," Susan said, heading back inside.

"I'll come and see him when we're through," Ajax said. His business with Hux could wait for now.

Walking along the path that led to the foaling barn, he and Fallon were stopped a couple of times, first by a rider and then a groom who wanted to say hi. She'd been popular with the team, and it had been a loss to his stables when she left.

"I miss this place," she said, gazing out over the hills and paddocks.

"Kentucky's pretty, too."

She nodded. "Dad still has half a dozen horses. Still rides every day."

Fallon's trainer father had enjoyed some success a couple of decades ago, which was how Fallon had found her way into the game.

"He always wanted you to ride in the Derby," Ajax recalled.

Fallon laughed. "I was never that good."

"You could have been if you'd kept going. Absolutely."

When she elbowed his ribs and laughed some more, Ajax got a funny feeling in his stomach. They'd always gotten on well. Common interests and parallel dreams. Which was hardly the case with Veda. But after yesterday, and particularly last night, they seemed to be overcoming their obstacles. Whenever they were together, he felt as if nothing else in the world existed. Like the only thing that mattered was making her happy.

But given the way she had cut him off at the knees in Barbados because of his innocent chat with that woman, how would Veda react if she saw him with Fallon when their relationship hadn't always been platonic?

Of course that was ancient history. Other than Griff, no one knew about their fling, and Ajax wouldn't go out of his way to mention it. Why upset Veda when there was absolutely nothing to worry about?

When they passed a stable hand leading a cream four-year-old, Ajax pulled him up.

"We need to check that left hind leg," he said, running a hand down the limb. "The hip's hiking when the leg hits the ground."

"The owner's already made up his mind about this one," the stable hand said.

Ajax frowned. "Made up his mind about what?"

"I thought he must've talked to you." The stable hand rubbed the horse's neck. "This guy's retiring. I'm about to load him up for the last time."

If a horse wasn't earning enough, an owner decided whether he would literally be put out to pasture, re-trained for a new career or...that other lesser-talked-about alternative that meant a one-way trip to Canada or Mexico. When he spoke to the owner to square the accounts, he would make an offer for the cream.

If it wasn't too late.

"Come on," he said to Fallon, focusing on the now. "I'll introduce you to Someone's Prince Charming. I'm backing him for a Triple Crown next year. He's a star, and just so smart and wanting to give his all."

He'd certainly known a few in his time, but Ajax loved that horse like he had loved no other.

Ajax stopped and turned around. Hux was trotting down the path, calling out his name. When he arrived, Hux gave Fallon a hug.

"Is this a professional visit?" he asked. "Looking to get back into your silks?"

Fallon gave him a good-humored grin. "My racing days are over."

"Well, we all want to hear what you're up to, so you're staying for dinner," Hux said. "No arguments."

Fallon caught Ajax's gaze and nodded. "I'd love to."

"Do you mind if I steal Ajax for a second? There's some business we need to discuss."

"Sure. I'll catch you up at the stables," she told Ajax, heading off.

When she was out of earshot, Hux pinned his son with a look. "Nice of you to show up today."

Wow. "I'm actually taking some time off. So sue me."

"Don't speak too soon."

Was he referring to the doping business and possible sanctions?

Man, he was so over this.

Ajax was walking away when Hux added, "She must be good."

Bristling, Ajax slowly turned back. "If you're talking about Veda—"

"It could be part of Darnel's plan, you know," Hux said, cutting in. "Make sure you're sidetracked while it all crumples down around me."

"Around *you*? Like I don't put my heart and soul into this place?"

"Not lately. This time of year, you need to be here, doing your job. Once I didn't have to tell you that."

"Right. Once all I did was beg for every crumb of approval you'd toss my way."

As a groom hurried past, eyes cast down, Hux lowered his voice. "You need to get your head on straight."

"Which means?"

"Priorities. Open your eyes to what could be happening here."

As Hux strode off, Ajax remembered how good Veda had felt in his arms last night, and then Fallon's recollection that Veda believed the Rawsons were unscrupulous, too. Perhaps that had come from her dislike of all things horse racing–related. It didn't mean that she would conspire to sell him out. Veda wouldn't do that.

No way, no how.

That evening, Veda was thinking she might have to leave a message when Ajax finally picked up.

"Hey there," he said, sounding beyond sexy.

"Hey, back." She set aside her laptop with images on the screen of teacup poodles available from rescue groups. "Just thought I'd check in and see how it went with your dad today."

"Hux is being a giant paranoid pain. I know we lost some business because of Booshang but…" He cursed under his breath. "I don't want to talk about any of that."

He sounded short, but she knew that wasn't about her. If she was in his position, she'd be stressed, too.

After an amazing night spent together here in the guesthouse, after the way he had supported her yesterday when Drake was being so, well, *Drake*, she was feeling even better about her relationship with Ajax. There might be a mountain of things standing in their way, but at least now she felt more secure about his feelings for her. Yes, he'd been a stud in the past, but that didn't mean he would always play the field. Hux had settled down eventually, hadn't he? So maybe this liaison wasn't as doomed as she had once thought.

"Did you speak with your dad today?" he asked.

"After we drove down to the hospital to get your car, I hung around for a while but he was still sulking, so I just dropped off those personal items I knew he'd need. He should be out in the next few days. I'll stay here until then."

She clicked on an image and sighed as a pair of adorable baby-blue puppy eyes melted her heart.

"You know, talking about Gus the other day got me thinking," she said.

"Gus who?"

"My little poodle, remember?" she reminded him. "He was just so loving and cuddly and cute. I've always wanted another one."

"Do it," Ajax said. "Animals are great company."

"As a matter of fact, I could use a little human company right now." She shut her laptop lid. "Wanna hang out?"

There was a beat of silence.

"Actually, we had a visitor from Kentucky drop in out of the blue. Someone I haven't seen in a while."

Veda let out a breath as all her built-up anticipation deflated. The way he had kissed her goodbye this morning, the promise he'd made about seeing her again… Well, naturally she had hoped…she'd assumed…

But she didn't want to act like a clinging vine.

"Oh, sure," she said, opening her laptop again. "I understand. Did you work together?"

"Uh-huh. A jockey."

"Would I know his name?"

"Fallon Kelly. She retired last year. Hux invited her to stay for dinner."

Last year, after a Drake rant about being swindled out of a Belmont Stakes blue ribbon by a Rawson horse, Veda had googled the story. Fallon Kelly was not only a talented jockey, she was a beautiful and obviously self-possessed woman. In the story's accompanying picture of Fallon with Ajax, she had radiated confidence. They obviously made a great team.

Putting aside a twinge of unease, Veda said, "Well, I'll let you get back to your guest then."

"I'll call tomorrow."

There was a long silence when something else needed to be said. *Have fun* didn't fit. *Be good* was even worse. *Love you* was way too much, too soon. Although she was heading in that direction, which could hardly be a surprise. It was what she had feared from the start. Now…it was too late to try to push those growing feelings aside.

Finally he said, "Sleep tight. And good luck with the puppy search. Can't wait to meet him."

Veda put down the phone on a sigh. If the Rawsons and Darnels weren't enemies, he might have invited her over to meet his guest. She would feel included rather than shunted aside. But it was only one night. This time tomorrow Fallon Kelly would be gone and Veda would be in Ajax's arms once again.

Thirteen

Finally Drake deigned to see his daughter.

Sitting up in his hospital bed, Veda's father was freshly shaved, wearing the pajamas she had dropped off for him two days earlier. Other than a bruised color around his eyes, he looked remarkably well and more than prepared to hold court.

As Veda entered the private room, he kept his stony gaze glued to hers, but he didn't speak, which was clearly a tactic to make her sweat. Although Veda's stomach was churning, she didn't shrink away.

Taking a seat by the window, she let the seconds tick by as he continued the stare-off. Finally, his lips sucked in and he cleared his throat.

"I'm dry. Pour me a water, please."

Veda got to her feet, poured a glass from a jug and handed it over.

"The doctor said you can leave in a couple of days," she said while he sipped.

"I can find my own way," he said, and then covered his mouth to cough.

"If you're not feeling up to it, don't rush yourself." Making sure she looked unconcerned, she crossed her arms. "I imagine you've spoken to the stable manager and trainers so things would be sorted out there."

"Did your boyfriend want you to ask me that?"

Veda was so taken aback, she almost fell sideways.

"I beg your pardon?"

"You invited him onto my property, didn't you?" he bit out. "My God, a Rawson in my house. Did you think I wouldn't find out? That my people wouldn't pass on what they saw?"

She hadn't noticed anyone around. Had Drake sent someone over from the stables to literally spy?

"It was bad enough," he went on, "that you spend time with a Rawson boy. But it had to be Ajax, didn't it? The biggest bastard of the pack."

An impulse shot through her: she wanted to leap over and slap his face. But she wouldn't stoop to his level. Instead, she bit her lip and, outwardly cool, simply tipped her head.

"He makes me happy," she told him, recalling her mother saying the same thing about her cowboy once upon a time.

Drake sneered. "He's even worse than his father.

Always charming the women. Seeing who he can fool. Rawson men don't care."

"Hux Rawson cared about the woman he married. I've been told that they loved each other deeply."

But this conversation was absurd.

"You've just survived a car accident, for God's sake. Can't you ever move on?"

Given his next question, clearly not.

"Married, you say?" Her father snickered. "Has Ajax asked you to marry him then?"

"Of course not!"

"Didn't think so."

Veda's hands fisted at her sides. "Bitterness destroys a person, Drake," she said. "It turns them rotten from the inside. It turns them bad."

Her father's eyes flashed at the same time he hurled his glass into a corner. As shards and water flew everywhere, Veda barely flinched. In fact, she stepped closer to the bed.

"Ajax is funny and laid-back. He's charming and brave. People are naturally attracted to men like that."

The corners of Drake's mouth pulled down more. His words were a harsh, hateful whisper. "You like to hurt me."

Veda withered. "You really are deluded."

When she was halfway out the door, he called out. "I'm going home tomorrow. Friday."

"Don't worry. I'll be gone."

"Veda."

She counted to ten before she turned back around. "What now?"

"I've changed my mind."

She looked at him hard. "Changed your mind about what exactly?"

"You can drive me home." He fluffed the sheet. "Be here by nine. Don't be late."

Lanie was lost in her thoughts when the cab driver kicked off a conversation.

"Said on the radio there's supposed to be a thunderstorm rolling in later today."

Glancing out the window, Lanie spotted a distant bank of clouds. "Rain is always nice."

"Oh, sure. As long as it's not too fierce." The driver added, "I have a vegetable patch at home so I take notice. Beets and peas and onions this year."

Lanie had gone back to her thoughts, trying to find a solution to her nagging problem, when the driver spoke again.

"Was it fine weather where you flew in from today? The rest of the state's supposed to be clear."

"I'm just back from visiting a friend in Germany."

"That's a long way to visit a pal," he said with a gravelly chuckle.

"We have a lot in common. And it was a special occasion."

Lanie had met her German friend at the Dressage World Championship in Tryon, North Carolina. She wasn't able to attend Lanie's birthday party, but with good reason. She'd been preparing for her wedding, at which Lanie had just been a bridesmaid.

Although not too many people knew, Lanie really

wanted a family someday, and the ceremony, which was held in the private courtyard of a centuries-old winery estate, had pulled all her romantic strings. Aside from the scenery and the couple's heartfelt vows, she couldn't help but remember the other special person she met during that trip to North Carolina. Kade Wilder had been a guest at one of the events held at the championships. He was handsome, articulate and passionate about running for Congress.

They had spent the night talking and later followed each other on social media. When Lanie had posted about her party, Kade had messaged he would be in town and would love to personally pass on his wishes. He had arrived late, but the dance they had shared was worth every second of the wait. As he'd held her in his arms, she had practically drowned in the dark blue pools of his eyes.

She wasn't the type to get goofy over a man, but her stomach had been filled with so many butterflies that night on the dance floor, and later when they had spoken alone. Perhaps the attraction was one-sided, though. Kade hadn't tried to kiss her that night, and he hadn't tried to contact her since.

"We'll be there in thirty," the driver said. "I've heard of Rawson's farm. They've had plenty of winners over the years."

"It was a great place to grow up, especially if you love horses."

Finding her phone, Lanie logged in to see whether Kade had posted anything since the last time she'd looked.

"So you're a Rawson kid?" the driver asked.

"I am."

"Must be hard right now with all those rumors about drugging and race-fixing floating around. Even money laundering. That's what some Darnel guy was hinting at on the radio this morning."

Lanie almost dropped her phone.

What the hell?

"Rawson's is one of the most reputable stables in the state. In the country."

The driver shrugged. "I'm sure it is, lady. Just sayin'."

Growling under her breath—at the situation, not the driver—Lanie swapped to another social media platform and swiped through the feed. She shouldn't be surprised that word of those doping allegations had leaked. People loved a scandal. But Hux and Ajax would have it sorted out soon enough. The Rawsons had overcome battles far tougher than this.

She stopped at a post from Veda. The caption indicated it was a view from Darnel Manor. The last time she and Veda had spoken was the morning after the party. Lanie had been stunned to learn that Ajax had scored that particular notch on his bedpost. Later, Veda had admitted that it hadn't been the first time.

Lanie had given her opinion on the subject, after which Veda had claimed that she wouldn't see Ajax again. Veda was a strong woman, but Ajax was a pro. If her brother set his mind to it, Lanie would bet her lucky saddle that Veda would fold.

Lanie focused on the photo again. If Veda was in

town, they should catch up. Veda might want to talk about Ajax. Lanie could use a sounding board, too. Was it better to file her feelings for Kade away under Obviously Not Happening, or should she be the one to reach out this time?

Lanie speed-dialed her friend. Veda answered with her usual direct style.

"Lanie. I'm glad you called."

"I've just flown in and caught your feed. Are you visiting with your dad?"

"Kind of. He's been in a car accident."

Lanie gasped. "God. Is he okay?" She didn't personally know the man, and if she did, she probably wouldn't like him, but she still felt for her friend.

"He was lucky," Veda explained. "He's in the hospital, though, so I'm house-sitting between visits."

Lanie sat forward, peering out the windshield down the road ahead. "I'm not far away. I should drop by."

There was a grin in Veda's voice when she replied, "You definitely should."

Ten minutes later, Lanie was out of the cab and enjoying Veda's welcoming hug. Lanie came right out and said it.

"I need to unpack about a man."

Veda groaned. "Same."

While they sat out back with a glass of wine and the sun arcing more toward the dark clouds traveling in from the north, Veda and Lanie played rock-paper-scissors to decide who went first.

Lanie won.

After listening to the whole gorgeous-but-MIA-man story, Veda wanted to highlight a point.

"I saw you two on the dance floor the night of your party. You were literally floating on air."

Looking off, Lanie swirled her wine in her glass. "I don't carry on with something if the feelings aren't right. I was beginning to think I was incapable of going all weak at the knees."

Veda raised her glass. "Guess no one is immune."

"Which brings us to my brother. He's the man you want to talk about, right?"

Veda filled her friend in. She didn't leave anything out, including playing *not* hard to get in Barbados, followed by the *getting jealous over probably nothing* episode at that dinner. She wrapped up with how Ajax had met her at the hospital after her father's accident and, later, had come back here to keep her company.

"He stayed over that night, and we've spoken on the phone since."

Lanie prodded. "But?"

"We haven't seen each other since Tuesday morning." This was Thursday afternoon. "After having a long weekend, I know he'd be busy with work, catching up. And there's that Booshang thing to deal with. A stewards' meeting is set for tomorrow. On top of that, some Rawson clients have removed their horses from the stables."

Lanie grunted, surprised, and then tossed back her hair. "They'll be back."

When Veda only bit her lip, Lanie frowned and tipped closer.

"Wait. You don't think Ajax actually doped that horse, do you?"

Veda admitted, "I wasn't sure at the start. I mean that kind of stuff happens all the time."

"Not at Rawson's."

"But that's not technically true. Paul Booshang was working for Ajax when he was caught."

Lanie paused before she got to her feet and looked out over the hills like she was daring them to point out the facts, too.

"Ajax and Jacob will clear our name," she said. "Dad'll make sure of it."

"Ajax says that Hux is giving him a hard time, too."

Lanie swung around. "Well, it seems as if I came home just in time then. Far too much testosterone flying around."

When Lanie grinned, Veda smiled, too. "*Way* too much testosterone," she agreed before she sobered again. "Maybe I'm being selfish or needy, but I wish Ajax could find a minute to come over and see me."

Lowering back down into her seat, Lanie made a suggestion. The most outlandish notion in the history of anything.

"Why don't you come over and see him instead?"

Veda almost spluttered her wine. "That's such a bad idea."

"Veda, it's my home, too. You're my friend, and I'm inviting you."

"Forget about Ajax maybe feeling like we're treading on his toes. My father was mentioned in connection to those allegations. I'm sure Hux doesn't want a Darnel shoved in his face any time soon."

Or ever.

"My father is an alpha male who's not afraid to stand up for what's right. But Veda, he's not a tyrant. In fact, he can be a big ol' pussycat where I'm concerned." She took Veda's hand. "I know there's talk about your father being involved in this somehow. But even if that's true, it's no reason to hold it against you."

"I'm not so sure."

"Spurned by association? My mother dated Drake but Hux didn't hold it against her, did he?"

Veda had to think that through. "I guess not..."

"So it's settled." She took Veda's glass and set it down. "You're driving me home."

Veda's throat convulsed. "I'm still not sure that's a good idea. He has that meeting tomorrow, don't forget."

Lanie's determined expression softened. "From what you told me, you and Ajax are getting over your hurdles. I'm sure he would appreciate the visit. In fact, he'll probably be blown away."

Veda had something else she needed to say. "I'm sorry I didn't tell you about me and Ajax after that first time."

Lanie waved it off. "We're friends. Not Siamese twins."

"But we've always been open with each other."

"That hasn't changed."

"I'm just saying...if you ever found anything out about Ajax...something that you might think I ought to know..."

When Lanie read between the obvious lines, her expression filled with understanding as well as conviction. "No secrets between friends. Promise."

Smiling, Veda nodded. "I promise, too."

After another long day taking care of business, including rolling calls from clients who were growing ever more curious about those pending test results, Ajax was happy to kick back. When Fallon arrived at his office, saying that she had brought along two saddled horses that were raring to go, Ajax didn't waste a moment pulling the whistle on quitting time.

He needed to stop thinking about the stewards' meeting set for tomorrow. Jacob would be sitting beside him, and Griff was taking a day off work to show his support for the team. Of course, Hux would be there, too. Frankly, Ajax wished he would simply stay the hell away.

Since their confrontation earlier in the week, Hux's mood had tanked even more. No one knew what the test results would reveal, or what penalties would be handed down. But, yes, mud tended to stick, particularly when Drake Darnel was slinging it around every opportunity he got, like in that absurd radio interview this morning.

Money laundering.

What a crock.

None of that impacted his feelings for Veda, but it had held him back from seeing more of her these past days. At this point in time, Hux didn't need the added aggravation of having his son flaunt the fact that he was sleeping with the enemy's daughter. Hux had never let Drake get under his skin before, either professionally or personally, but this was a whole other ball game.

The big question was whether Darnel was shoveling his crap onto the Rawsons to divert attention from his own part in this doping episode. If that was the case, when would the truth be revealed?

Ajax was glad that Fallon had accepted Hux's invitation to stay on a few days. She understood the industry; whenever he vented about this, she was only ever supportive. And she helped in other ways, Ajax thought as he stepped outside and glanced at the clouds rolling in.

She came along on his rounds and helped out with track work. Best of all, she managed to bring the occasional smile to Hux's dour face.

Once those results were in, Ajax thought as Fallon spurred on her horse through the open paddock gate, everyone would be free to get on with their lives. He could properly pick up with Veda where they had left off. And if Hux wasn't happy about that state of affairs, too damn bad.

Ajax would always love and respect his father, but these past weeks had put a different spin on how he viewed their relationship. He'd given his heart, blood and soul to this place. Irrespective of those test results, he needed a partnership contract now. Tomorrow after the meeting, he would give Hux the news.

"Hey, Jax, I'll race ya!"

Fallon, who was handling that chestnut two-year-old like the pro she was, was already springing into a gallop. As she bolted off, throwing a goading look over her shoulder, Ajax swung into his saddle, and Someone's Prince Charming took off after them. Fallon was such a natural; hanging up her silks seemed a waste. Which brought to mind the other reason he was glad she had stayed. Having her own riding school was cool, but having their horse wear the Kentucky Derby's rose blanket next year would be monumental. And she, along with the Prince, had the goods to deliver.

Fallon just beat him to the oak at the top of the next slope. As her horse snorted and lowered his head to tear off some grass, Ajax pulled up, too. Breathing in air scented with approaching rain, he gazed out over the hills he called home.

"I'm going to miss this place," Fallon said as the sun disappeared behind the bank of rolling clouds.

"You don't have to go," Ajax said, leaning on his saddle's horn while she dismounted.

"I have a life to get back to."

"Don't you miss the one you left behind?"

Fallon swept up a wildflower and twirled the stem. "We've talked about that. I made a decision to move on. I don't regret it."

Climbing down to join her, Ajax asked, "Not even a teensy bit?"

"I need to do something different. Something for me."

"But you loved being a jockey," he said, stealing the flower and slotting the stem behind her ear.

"The truth is I did it for my father. It was always his dream."

Ajax blinked. "I didn't know that."

"As a boy, Dad dreamed of bringing home a Derby win, but he was never the right build to ride. I was."

"Winning the Kentucky Derby..." Ajax playfully punched her arm. "You could still do that. I have the ride right here."

While Ajax stroked his horse's warm, strong neck, Fallon searched his eyes for a long moment.

"Ajax, are you trying to talk *me* into staying or you?"

Muscles in his chest locked before he reevaluated those hills, which were fast becoming covered in shadow rather than sunlight.

Shaking his head, remembering how it used to be, Ajax growled. "I wish this had never happened." Booshang's behavior that day and his ridiculous allegations had turned the world upside down.

"This all could be a blessing in disguise," Fallon said. "A new opportunity for you. A new start."

If, or rather when, Hux signed that partnership agreement... "Yeah. I suppose it could."

"So you'll consider my suggestion."

"What suggestion?"

"That you help me with my riding school. We spoke about it the other night."

Over dinner. But they'd been joking around.

"I'm not saying give up what you do here, just lend a hand when you can. I think we could have fun." Fallon's smile changed as she adjusted the flower in her hair. "I think we could be happy."

A lightning bolt ignited the sky, cutting a jagged line through the churning clouds. Seconds later, an almighty clap of thunder split the air. Whinnying, Fallon's horse reared up, then charged back down the hill toward the safety of its stall. Ajax caught the Prince's reins as another bolt struck and an even worse clap shook the ground. The next second, hard rain began to fall.

Ajax jumped up into his saddle then threw out his hand to Fallon. "Want a lift?"

She caught his hand. "Bless your heart!"

She swung up behind him and they lit a trail back down the hill.

With rain hitting his face, Ajax let out a whoop. This was what life was about. Feeling free...even reckless. Like you could do anything when you decided nothing would hold you back.

Fallon was an amazing woman—beautiful, talented. He'd known that when she'd won the Stakes as well as later, when they had slipped away to be alone. He had loved catching up with her these past days.

But he had seen the look in her eyes a moment ago. When she'd said they could be happy, she was talking about more than working together on a riding school. If he had stepped into her space...if he'd kissed her... she wouldn't have pulled away.

But Fallon wasn't the one he wanted right now, and when they were under cover, he would be clear in letting her know exactly that.

Veda was driving up the Rawsons' private road, heading toward that fateful bend, when the heavens opened up and dumped big-time. As the sudden rain smashed against the windshield, Lanie readjusted her seat belt.

"This is one serious summer shower."

Veda switched on the wipers and shifted closer to the wheel. "Reminds me of the rain the night of your party."

"When your car spun out."

"Right here, actually," Veda said as the SUV rounded the corner and her stomach lurched.

"You must've been happy to see Ajax charging down to rescue you."

Remembering it all very well, Veda wanted to smile. But other older memories made her shudder instead.

"I wonder what would have happened," Veda said as the vehicle climbed toward the house, "if it hadn't rained that night."

Lanie shrugged. "What's meant to be is meant to be."

Then the belting rain stopped as quickly as it had started, and the guest parking area appeared before them. As Veda pulled into a spot, she noticed some movement on an adjacent hill. Soaked through, Ajax was riding toward the house on the back of a magnificent-looking steed.

With his hair flying back and his shirt wet through, tugging against all those gorgeous muscles, he had never looked so handsome. So capable and in charge. She couldn't wait to feel those arms around her again.

Veda was hurrying to shut down the engine and jump out when, beside her, Lanie groaned out an expletive. Her eyes were bulging like she'd swallowed a toad. A chill rippled over Veda's skin as she reached across to hold her friend's shoulder.

"Lanie? God, what's wrong?"

"Nothing. Not a thing."

Lanie pasted on a limp smile that only made Veda worry more. She looked out through the windshield again as another chill swept over her. Ajax was bringing his horse to a showy stop. Someone was hooked up behind him. As he helped the other rider down, the woman looked up at him as if no one else compared.

As if he was the best.

Veda's scalp started crawling. She didn't want to jump to conclusions, be overdramatic. But come on. She wasn't a fool.

Without taking her eyes off the woman, she asked Lanie, "Is it someone from his past or someone new?"

Lanie exhaled. "You and Ajax should probably talk."

Veda clenched her jaw and drew down a big breath. *No secrets between friends.*

"If you know anything..."

Lanie shut her eyes and dropped her chin. "Griff mentioned something last year..."

Ajax was dismounting. He'd seen her car and was heading over with an uncharacteristically measured stride. She felt strangely hypnotized by the way those wet jeans clung to his thighs and his narrowed gaze held hers.

"What's her name?"

"Fallon Kelly," Lanie replied. "She's a jockey. Or was. She'd hung up her whip last I heard."

Veda felt as if she was folding in on herself and

melting away. The surprise guest had stayed on longer than a night. Longer than Ajax had said she would or had mentioned in his calls.

By the time Ajax reached the car, the shock was ebbing. In its place, Veda felt those familiar fingers curl around her throat at the same time her brain began to shut down. But she needed to speak with Ajax. No games. No blinders. She simply wanted the truth.

Getting out of the car, she took in Ajax's plastic grin and the way his big shoulders in that chambray shirt slouched just a bit as he shook out his wet hands. He went to take a step closer, but then blinked and rocked back on his boot heels instead.

"Well, this is a double surprise," he said, acknowledging Lanie, who was out of the car now, too. "Veda." He jerked a thumb over his shoulder. "I mentioned Fallon Kelly was staying over. She used to ride for us."

Still standing by that magnificent horse, obviously realizing that Veda was Ajax's latest squeeze, Fallon sent over a half-hearted wave. Veda recognized her face from that story she'd read about her online. While Lanie joined Fallon, Veda and Ajax simply stood there, drilling into each other's eyes.

"You want to come down to the office?" he asked her.

"I'm not holding you up?" Veda replied.

His eyebrows drew together before he nodded toward the path. They walked side by side, neither saying a word the entire way. When they got inside, they moved through to his private office, and he shut the door.

She wanted him to talk first. Would he try to say

this was completely innocent, or that it was all in her head? Maybe the time had come where he would simply say that he felt bad about them not working out. That would definitely fit.

"I know what you're thinking," he said.

"What's that?" she asked.

"That Fallon and I... That something's going on." He gave an exaggerated shrug. "We're just friends."

"If I could make an observation..."

He exhaled. "Go ahead."

"I would put my money on her wanting way more than friendship."

Veda almost expected him to deny knowing it, too. But he only searched her eyes as his bristled jaw worked from side to side. Veda's stomach went into free fall.

"We went for a ride," he said. "There was a clap of thunder. Fallon's horse freaked and galloped home. That's all there is to it."

Veda's throat was blocked with emotion. At the same time, she felt something akin to relief. This was really over. He didn't want to admit that he and Fallon Kelly had slept together in the past. And it sure as hell seemed like they were sleeping together now.

"Okay," she said.

His eyes narrowed. "Okay?"

"It doesn't matter."

"I'm getting the impression that it matters a lot."

She tried to ignore the tears pounding away at the backs of her eyes, threatening to break through.

"The bottom line is that I don't trust you."

His eyes grew darker as the line of his mouth hardened. But his voice remained level. She guessed he might actually be hurt. The Stud always did the dumping, not the other way around.

"So I'm the only one who's supposed to embrace blind faith?"

She frowned. "What the hell are you talking about?"

"The Booshang fiasco. I keep defending you when other people think you might be involved."

Talk about deflection. How dare he throw that other stuff in her face now.

He cut her off before she got to the door.

"We need to talk, Veda."

Her unshed tears kept building up, but she held them back.

"I have nothing more to say."

"I don't know what you want from me." He drove both hands through his damp hair. "Galloping down that hill, I swear I was only thinking of you."

"Don't worry." She shoved past him. "You'll get over it."

Veda hated to think just how quick.

Fourteen

The next day, the stewards' meeting was over in record time.

As Ajax left the building, he didn't have a chance to rehash the findings with his family before a tidal wave of reporters descended. There were TV cameras crowding him in while microphones got shoved in his face.

"How do you feel about the decision?" one reporter asked.

"What's your next move?" asked another.

"Clients have left Rawsons," someone cried out from the back of the mob. "How badly has this discredited your name?"

In his faultless attorney style, Jacob stepped forward and spoke for the family.

"This meeting was a courtesy to let Ajax Rawson know that samples taken from Someone's Prince Charming confirmed that no State Gaming Commission regulations were violated with regard to illegal drugs, medications or other substances. Furthermore, we would like to make clear that Mr. Rawson was not aware of Paul Booshang's questionable actions on the day under investigation."

A different reporter from a national network got her question in.

"Why did Paul Booshang implicate you, Ajax?"

Ajax stepped forward while his family arced around him. "You'd have to ask him. It seems bizarre and a total waste of time to me."

"Today Booshang implicated another big stable owner in multiple past misdeeds dating back decades," the same reporter said. "Will Drake Darnel be investigated?"

Hux fielded the question. "We can't speak for anyone else." He clapped Ajax on the shoulder. "We're just glad to get back to business as usual."

There were a few more questions asked and answered before Jacob stepped in again and closed the session.

"Well done," Hux said, shaking both his sons' hands as the reporters began to drift away. "And now that we're all law-and-ordered out, I suggest we put on our feed bags."

Wearing a smart pantsuit, Lanie piped up, "There's a new place opened around the corner. Grape pie's on the menu, I hear." She found Susan's gaze. "Not anywhere near as good as yours, of course. But it is the man of the hour's favorite."

Ajax loved grape pie almost as much as he loved the support his family was showing him. He couldn't have been more pleased with the outcome. But for once he wasn't particularly hungry. He was thinking about Veda. He couldn't get her out of his mind.

Jacob was hugging the women goodbye. "I gotta go. I promised Buddy and Tea I'd cook my world's best ever spaghetti tonight. Pasta from scratch. Sauce to die for."

Susan planted a big kiss on his cheek. "You need to give me the recipe."

"And we need to see the rest of the family up here again soon," Hux added as he drew Susan close. "There's nothing better."

Clearly Hux and Susan were in love—had been for many years. There was a familiarity and trust that radiated whenever they were together, and it didn't matter that they weren't as young as they once were. That kind of love just grew and grew. It was real and it was lasting.

"I'm going to shoot off, too," Griff said, checking his wristwatch.

"Big date tonight?" Jacob asked, nudging Ajax in the ribs as if to say, *We know this dude's game.*

"As a matter of fact...none of your business." Griff gave a wink as he headed off.

Which left four to enjoy that new place Lanie had recommended.

"Ajax, I need to apologize," Hux said as the women walked off ahead of them.

Ajax wasn't sure this was the right place or time.

"We can talk later, Dad."

"It's been weighing on my mind...how I expected too much of you, and even learned to depend on you. You're right. I don't show nearly enough gratitude for what you do. I haven't truly acknowledged how much you've sacrificed."

Ajax felt as if his chest just puffed out ten inches. He and Hux had said some things to each other they shouldn't have. It was good to hear his father open up this way.

"We wouldn't be nearly as successful," Hux went on, "if it weren't for all the hours you put in every week."

"Well, I love taking care of my team."

Susan was calling out, "You guys coming?"

Hux replied, "Be right there." Then he caught Ajax's gaze again and gave a definitive nod. "Jacob has his career. Griff and Lanie, too. And you, Ajax, have made a real name for yourself in this industry, not only as a trainer and businessman but as a gentleman."

Ajax ran a finger around the inside of his collar. "I wouldn't go that far."

"People enjoy your company. They want to work with you. Yes, we've had some losses these past weeks, but that won't take away from your legacy."

Legacy? "I'm not that old, am I?"

"Well, you're old enough for this." Hux reached into his jacket's inner pocket and drew out a folded document. "You deserve this, son. I should have taken care of it sooner."

When Ajax unfolded the paperwork, his stomach did a flip. He could barely believe his eyes. "This is a partnership agreement."

"Between you and me for the farm."

Ajax coughed out a laugh. This was precisely what he'd wanted. What he had decided to demand as long overdue. Inside he was kicking his heels, pumping both fists, because he was legitimately happy.

Yep.

He really was.

"It needs your signature," Hux explained as Ajax handed the contract back.

"Sure." He blew out a shaky breath over a smile and added, "Thanks. I really mean that."

"I know you do." Hux hesitated. "But I can see you're focused on something else right now."

Ajax rolled back his shoulders, shook his head. "You don't want to know."

"Let me guess. Veda Darnel." When Ajax nodded, Hux's expression deepened. "I owe you an apology there, too. I attacked that girl's character when, of course, she wasn't involved in the Booshang mess. Veda Darnel is important to you. I should have given that more consideration before running my mouth off. I was just pissed at her father shooting *his* mouth off to the press…pointing fingers…"

A reporter rushed over—the same guy who had asked about their next move.

"A heads-up," the reporter said. "We're all shooting over to get a statement from Darnel."

"You're out of luck," Ajax said. "Drake Darnel is in the hospital."

"Negative. My sources say he got out this morning. I'm not sure that he knows he's been implicated in the wrongdoing today." The reporter was striding away. "We're about to find out."

"They never let up," Hux said, removing his hat to dab his brow with a monogrammed handkerchief. "Hell, I almost feel sorry for Drake having to face it alone, and with no warning."

Ajax didn't care about Drake Darnel. As that reporter jumped into a news van and sped off, he was thinking about the one person who didn't deserve a grilling. The only person he cared about right now.

Veda.

Earlier that morning, when Veda had arrived, the doctor had yet to finish his rounds and give her father a green light to leave. In the waiting room, Veda had taken the time to reaffirm her decision, effective as of today.

To say Drake Darnel was a difficult man was an understatement. This week he had provoked not one but two significant disagreements. Rarely did he show that he cared. As far as fatherly affection was concerned, he'd missed practically every class. But that was on him.

Veda had her own life now.

The drive home from the hospital had been strained.

Now as Drake walked into the house and headed for the kitchen, Veda took in his lanky figure. He was getting older...more gray hair and even more impatience. When she was a little girl, of course she had respected him. Growing up, she had no choice but to endure his miserable moods. Even as an adult, she had taken his BS. But now, if Drake wasn't on board with the whole mutual respect thing—if he wanted to continue with this crazy controlling crap—then she didn't need to be around him anymore.

She was done.

In the kitchen, he found his favorite Wedgwood cup and saucer. After the water boiled, he brewed his pungent green tea without a word or a look. She knew the drill. Her father dished out his silent treatment as often as sharks shed teeth.

As he lifted the cup, he sniffed and said, "Thank you for collecting me this morning."

Veda's reply was hollow. Automatic.

"You're welcome."

"The doctor said that I'm well enough to drive again now."

Meaning he didn't need her to taxi him around in one of his many cars housed in that huge, pristine garage.

Wonderful.

He took his time slicing a lemon and squeezing just enough into the brew before his gaze lifted to meet hers for the first time that day.

"This hasn't been a good week," he said.

"Tell me about it."

He grunted and squeezed some more lemon.

"Veda, are you still seeing that man?"

She stiffened. Firstly, she didn't want to think about Ajax right now. She wished she never had to think about him again. Secondly, her father needed to back off.

"I won't discuss Ajax Rawson with you," she replied.

"I think we need to talk about it," he said.

"I really don't."

"Come into the living room and we'll sit down."

As he moved toward her, Veda's patience expired and she held up her hand for him to stop.

"I won't do this anymore."

He frowned. "Do what?"

"I need to walk away. I mean *really* walk away. I should have done it a long time ago."

His brow furrowed before he scratched an ear and set his cup and saucer back down on the counter.

"I need to show you something," he said. "Something I see every day and yet never want to acknowledge."

Veda pushed out a heavy breath. "You're talking in riddles." Trying to manipulate her.

"A riddle... I suppose it is. Maybe we can solve it together."

Veda narrowed her eyes at him. She hadn't heard him use this tone before, or this tactic. "You aren't making any sense."

"Why don't you come and see for yourself?" When she continued to study him, trying to work out the trap, his eyebrows pinched before a small smile hooked one side of his mouth.

"Please, Veda?" he asked.

She couldn't remember a time when Drake had looked anything close to vulnerable. Whatever this riddle was, she had to see it.

She followed him through to the den, a large, well-appointed room with its own library, wet bar and assortment of fine art, including a full-sized bronze horse sculpture at the dead center of the room. Drake went to stand behind his ultra-tidy desk and waited for her to join him. When they were side by side, he slid open the top left-hand drawer, reached inside and pulled out three items...a pair of gold wedding rings and a photograph. A family photograph from when Veda was a little girl, prior to going to school.

He laid the rings in his palm and flipped over the photo—the inscription on the back read, "Veda's three!"—before placing it faceup on the desk. In awe, she took in the image of father, mother and daughter sitting on the chesterfield in the living room. Drake was so young, with dark hair and no scowl lines. With her cheek pressed against Veda's, her beautiful mom was beaming. The room was packed with people smiling for the camera or looking adoringly at the lucky girl with her striking cloud of red curls. Drake was holding a kids' picture book—a birthday gift, Veda assumed.

As she let the image sink in, Veda's throat ached with emotion. There was gratitude that she had once known this kind of support coupled with a near-desperate longing to know it again. She was still digesting the fact that

Drake had kept those wedding rings and this happy family snapshot when he drew a fourth item from the drawer. It was an old book.

The one in the photo.

"I wanted you to grow up to be smart and happy," he said, focusing on the cartoon barn animal scene on the book's cover.

Absorbing every detail of the cover, with its two horses, cow, three pigs and fluffy little dog, Veda got this warm, rippling feeling. She couldn't be sure, but it was so similar to the picture she'd had in her mind for so long...an image of how her own animal farm might look.

Her father cleared his throat but then studied the photograph again with a smile she had never seen on him before...like he not only remembered but also cherished having had that joy in his life.

"I spent practically all my time on the business," he said, "making sure you were both well provided for... that you could grow up with everything you needed and deserved. The trouble started the day after this party. She asked me to spend more time with you both. As the years went by, her patience turned into irritation and, ultimately, despair."

Veda picked up the musty-smelling photo and looked into her mother's smiling eyes. So many times she remembered her saying that she had only ever wanted three things: a happy child, a nice home and a good husband. Was that too much to ask?

"The more your mom insisted I put work second," he went on, "the more I retreated and looked back, clutching on to something—some*one*—who had never truly been mine. To take my mind off fixing a real problem, being less selfish, I began to focus on that aspect of my life. I picked and picked until I felt it like a scab on my heart."

He was talking about the woman Hux Rawson had fallen in love with and married. The mother Ajax had lost around the same time Veda's own mom had died.

"I was an uncompromising fool, stuck in my ways." Drake eyes were glistening. "I threw it all away."

Veda had never heard her father speak like this before...with insight and humility. Like a human being rather than a cracked and bitter shell.

"I saw you slap her once," she said.

He cringed like he remembered it well. "She had stopped talking to me. Stopping caring altogether. I thought she might have someone else." He shook his head hard. "I was wrong. There's no excuse. None."

Veda had half expected him to deny the entire incident, so she got something else off her chest. "I can't remember you ever really talking to me."

"I kept it all in. Blocked everyone out. And this week, I've pushed you even further away. I know if I don't change, and change now, I'll lose you again, and this time for good." Holding that book to his chest, he turned more toward her and lowered his chin. "I don't want that to happen. Veda. It's hard for me to say, but—" he swallowed deeply "—I need your help."

This conversation just kept getting weirder. "You want *my* help?"

"I see from your blog, you're a bit of an expert at that."

Veda's mouth dropped open. She must have heard wrong.

"You read my blog?"

"Every post. It's to the point. Extremely informative." His eyes shone as he smiled. "I haven't told you for so many years. I'm proud of you, Veda. I know your mother would be proud of you, too."

Those words… The night of that party, she remembered Hux saying them to Lanie.

The right thing to do was wrap her arms around her father and tell him everything was forgiven…to let go of the uncertainty, the fear and all the frustration. Letting go was a choice, after all. But she needed time to come to terms with this sudden change of heart and accept that her father might actually, well, love her.

So she held off on gushing. Instead, she returned her father's smile and nodded as if to say, *Let's see what happens from here. Fingers crossed.*

A speculative gleam appeared in his eye.

"Now we really do need to speak about Ajax Rawson."

She groaned. "Dad, can we not?"

"I was only going to say that we should have him over for dinner sometime." He anticipated her reaction. "Yes, it will be a little awkward. The Rawsons and Darnels are far from friends. I've done some things I'm ashamed of, particularly this week. I'm not sure Ajax would even accept an invitation. But I can try, Veda. *We* can try."

If the offer had come a week earlier, she would have considered it. But her on-again, off-again relationship with Ajax had been permanently laid to rest. Any notion of extending olive branches between the families was too late.

So, should she let her father know about the breakup? Would his eyes fill with sympathy—support—or would he simply say *I told you so*?

The sound of the knocker hitting the front door echoed through the house. But her father didn't react. He had more to say.

"How does a man who has lost what's most important get it back?" he asked. "That's the riddle."

She didn't have the whole answer, but said, "He starts by saying I'm sorry and meaning it."

Drake hung his head before finding her eyes again. "I'm so sorry, Veda. Sorry for driving your mother away. Sorry for putting up that wall and not appreciating what I had."

The knocker sounded again.

Veda swept away a tear before it fell. "We should probably get that."

He tried on a smile. "To be continued, then?"

Before she could answer, Veda's ears pricked up to a different sound. "Do you hear that?"

Drake's eyes narrowed as he looked out the den's window, which gave a partial view of the front of the house. "There are vans pulling up." He headed for the door. "I'll go see what's happening."

Veda set the photograph down and told him, "I'm going with you."

Out in front of the Darnel mansion, the Rawson truck skidded to a stop. With Hux riding shotgun—

Lanie and Susan had decided to stay in town and leave this showdown to the men—Ajax had arrived here in record time but, unfortunately, not soon enough.

Reporters were congregated on the lawn, the same pack Jacob had handled so well earlier. Cameras were pointed like cannons at the front door, and questions were being thrown like knives. Facing the onslaught, standing at the center of his extravagant stone porch, Drake Darnel looked completely blindsided.

Ajax didn't care about Drake. Only Veda. She was standing beside her father, chin high, loyal to the bitter end.

Ajax threw open the car door, growling, "I'm going to save my girl."

"This all ends now," Hux replied, growling, too. "*All* of it."

Together, father and son strode up and cut through the media mob. Ajax was ready to tell them all to back the hell off and go home. But then Hux did something downright extraordinary. Something that had Ajax doubting his own eyes and ears.

Hux trotted up those porch steps. When he came to stand beside his old enemy, Drake's shocked expression deepened and Veda's eyes practically popped out of her skull. Then, turning to confront the mob, Hux waved his arms. When the barrage of questions quietened, he took a breath while Drake and Veda gaped on.

"My family spoke with you people earlier," Hux said. "You all know the score on those dud test results. As you are all obviously aware, this morning

Paul Booshang, a former employee, went on to implicate Drake Darnel in similar illegal activities."

"Mr. Darnel!" a reporter called out. "Sir, what is
your relationship with Paul Booshang?"

"Has the State Gaming Commission been in touch
regarding this matter?" asked another.

Drake took a halting step forward. "The Darnel
Stables… I have never…would…never…"

Hux edged closer to Drake's side and, catching his
gaze, tried to share a stalwart smile.

"Let me be honest here. These stables are among the
best and most reputable in the state," Hux said. "In the
country." His voice took on a solemn tone. "Our families have known each other many years. I would like to
go on the record as standing alongside our neighbors
against these baseless allegations."

Ajax was watching Veda watching Hux. She looked
like a child tasting ice cream for the first time—there
was a second of surprise quickly followed by delight.

Hux went on. "Mr. Darnel has returned from the hospital only a short time ago. I'm sure you all agree, we
need to walk it back and respect his privacy right now."
He offered a meaningful smile to Drake. "It's time we
all moved on."

Talk about taking the high road.

As the reporters and cameramen drifted off toward
their vehicles, Ajax made his way up the porch steps.
He wasn't sure what he was going to say to Hux, let
alone Drake; this morning had certainly been one for
the books.

But more importantly, he needed to talk with Veda.

The last time they had spoken, she hadn't pulled any punches. He didn't have what she needed, and he would move on soon enough.

Ajax hadn't agreed then, and he didn't agree now. He needed one more chance to have her hear why.

Hux put out his arm to welcome his son as he climbed the steps. "Drake, I don't know if you've had the pleasure of meeting my boy."

As the other man's watery gaze narrowed, Ajax held his breath. Drake knew he had been seeing Veda. Given Drake's screwy way of looking at the world, he might view that as stealing his daughter, just as Hux had "stolen" the woman Drake had loved so many years ago.

But now Drake only surrendered a genuine smile and put out his hand.

"I'm pleased to meet you... Ajax, isn't it?"

Ajax's knees almost buckled. He had to be dreaming.

But when Drake's smile not only held but grew, Ajax accepted the fact that miracles did happen. Which was great news, because he sure as hell could use another one right about now.

There was a brief exchange about this morning's meeting and Hux's handling of the media before Drake invited them all inside for a cool drink. Ajax had felt Veda's eyes on him the entire time. Had this unfolding scene softened her stand against him? Ready or not, time to find out.

"A cool drink would be nice," he told Drake before focusing on Veda. "But I'd like to speak with your daughter first, if that's all right."

After an awkward beat, in which Drake and Veda

exchanged looks, Drake headed for the open front door, tossing over his shoulder, "Huxley, shall we?"

When he and Veda were alone, Ajax tried on a *well, here we all are smile* while she scooped her hair back behind her ear, searching his eyes, looking more beautiful than ever before.

"I appreciate you and Hux coming today," she said. "We were totally unprepared for reporters."

"They'd just finished with us when we got word they were on their way here."

She titled her head. "So, congratulations on the test results."

"Yeah, well, it was an experience, and not without consequences."

"Have any more clients bailed?"

"One. But we've had a lot of support, as well."

She nodded. "Full steam ahead then."

"Which brings me to some other news. You remember how I wanted Hux to consider a partnership? I was saving the discussion until this was all over, but Dad was a step ahead of me. Right after the meeting this morning, he presented me with a document—fifty-fifty."

Her eyebrows edged up. "Bet you couldn't find a pen fast enough."

A week ago, that would have been the smart bet. As it turned out, he had handed the contract back, leaving it unsigned. For now.

When Veda slid a look toward the front door, he anticipated her next words. She would either suggest that they join their fathers or, more likely, that she would leave the men alone to talk. Neither option worked. He wanted more time with her alone. He needed to somehow make this right.

He spoke again before she could.

"So your dad got the all clear from the doctor?"

She nodded an unusually long time as if she wasn't sure if she should fill him in more.

"Actually, Dad and I had a discussion this morning," she finally said. "A real talk like I can't remember ever happening before."

"That's *huge*. Seems like it's a day for progress."

"Well, it's a start." She surrendered a smile. "I think a good start."

There was another loaded silence during which Ajax thought he saw a glimmer of anticipation in her eyes…a spark of *Say the right thing now and maybe I'll agree to see where this goes*. He had nothing to lose and pretty much everything to gain.

He'd get the tricky part out of the way first.

"Fallon's gone. She wanted me to pass on that she's sorry if she caused any trouble between you and me."

Other than crossing her arms, Veda gave no response. Not a word.

He forced the admission out. "I want to tell you that years ago, she and I spent a night together. Just one."

"I know."

"You…know?"

"Lanie told me."

"How did she—?"

"Griff."

He grunted. "So much for a brother's confidence."

"Oh, Ajax, I'm sure he's not the only one who knew."

He got back to the point. "Now Fallon is a friend," he said. "That's it. Friend. Period."

When Veda continued with the bland stare, he pushed on. He could feel his time running out. He needed to act, bring her close, show her just how he felt.

"Veda, I want to see you again."

Her jaw tightened before she shook her head.

No?

"Our fathers have put aside their differences," he said. "Can't we at least try to do the same?"

"I'm glad everyone's talking again. Dad and Hux. Me and my father. You and your dad."

He stepped forward, close enough to feel her warmth and for her to feel his.

"I'm way more interested in the two of us," he said.

She shook her head again.

"It's just… I feel very strongly about this," he went on. "About us."

"I know it's hard when you're so used to winning."

Every muscle in his body tensed. He had never known a woman like her. She never gave him a pass.

And then, as if she wanted to prove him wrong, she unfolded her arms and made a concession.

"I believe you about Fallon Kelly," she said.

He sparked up. "You do?"

When she looked almost disappointed, like she thought he was surprised that he had pulled the wool over her eyes, he took it down a notch.

"It's the truth. Veda, I would never do that to you."

She seemed to gather her thoughts before moving to the railing. When he joined her, her eyes were narrowed on the horizon like she was trying to see into the future. Or maybe back into the past.

"I'm not a fan of cowboys," she said. "Particularly the smooth-talking kind."

"You've made that pretty clear."

"Do you want to know why? The truest, deepest, most terrifying reason?"

As she faced him, he searched her resigned expression and nodded. "I really do."

"You know that my mother died in a car accident," she began.

"That was the word at the time."

"I was in the back seat."

He straightened as his stomach pitched. "God, Veda...were you hurt?"

"Not a scratch." Her grin was wry. "Isn't that something?"

More than ever, he wanted to reassure her somehow. But the best way to do that now was to sit tight and listen.

"After Mom left my dad, she hooked up with a man. A cowboy with a silver tongue. Or at least where my mother was concerned. Dad didn't keep in touch as such, but he sent money. Lots of it. Her cowboy was as sweet as he needed to be to get Mom to pay all the bills, including his gambling debts."

Ajax shuddered. He knew about Veda's problems with her dad and dyslexia. But this story was shaping up to be even worse.

"There were times when I was alone with him. He was nice until he started drinking. When he found out

I couldn't read that well, he liked to put me down. He'd make out like he was joking, calling me Dumbo, flapping his hands at the sides of his head."

Oh, Ajax was mad now. Was this asshole still alive? He wanted to track him down and teach him a lesson about picking on someone his own size.

"The night of the accident," Veda went on, "he was drinking from a flask with a pair of bull's horns etched into the tin. Mom was driving. He wanted to see Vegas, so Vegas it was. He'd never been mean to me in front of her before. Only ever sweet like he was with her, even when she accused him of being with another woman. *It's all in your head, darlin'. I would never do that to you.* But he told me once—said it straight-out—Mom was just his latest."

Ajax felt as if he were shrinking into the floor. The link was obvious.

But he wasn't that cowboy. He wasn't that kind of man.

He dug his hands deeper into his pockets. "You didn't tell your mom how he was with you?"

"I wanted to, but I didn't want to take her happiness away. She was so in love with the guy."

The absolute wrong guy.

While Ajax ground his teeth, Veda continued her story.

"We were in the car that night when he started on about my grades. I needed to try harder, he said. Do better. Then he called me Dumbo, softly at first, but getting louder. Growing meaner."

Veda's hands were laced together so tight, the knuckles were white.

"I didn't want to cry," she said. "I wanted to tell him to shut up. That he wasn't any better than me. But I was frozen...couldn't get the words out. Mom was ripping into him, though. Telling him to back off or get out."

Ajax felt sick to his stomach. There really were some first-class pricks in the world. Men who got their kicks from hurting kids and women. Lowlifes who had zero respect for themselves or anyone else.

"I was sitting in the back seat," Veda said, "throat closed, only choked sobs getting out. Then...all I remember is the bull horns on that flask and the oncoming headlights getting closer through the rain."

Ajax had heard enough. He brought Veda close and held her until she had finished shaking.

"The thing is," she went on, "when we lived here, I blamed myself for my mother being unhappy so much of the time. She wanted to keep the family together. I was the reason she stayed so long. And, of course, I blamed myself for the accident. For her death. She'd been distracted, trying to protect the dumb, mute weirdo who had never learned to defend herself."

Ajax dredged up a heavy smile. "But, boy, you can stand up for yourself now."

She straightened. "I know who I am. Even if it's hard sometimes, I know what I need to feel good about myself, and I can't afford to ever go back." Cupping his cheek, she searched his eyes and told him, "Ajax, not even for you."

Fifteen

Since that afternoon two weeks ago when she and Ajax Rawson had said goodbye for good, Veda had fallen into a slump. She had gotten involved with the wrong man and fallen in love. Now she was paying the price.

Today, after seeing off a new client at the door of her Jersey condo, Veda pulled up her sleeves and made a decision. She needed to regain a sense of control and, as nervous as she was about it, she thought she knew how. Time to step up, put it out there and reclaim that final piece of her power.

Veda opened her laptop and pulled up her Best Life Now blog on the screen. Over the years, she had discussed life's many challenges here: family, health, education and, of course, relationship issues. But this morning's post would go deeper and hopefully help even more.

I always try to be honest, Veda wrote under the header "A Life Coach's Best Advice." *That's the way to build trust in relationships and get good results. Except I haven't been completely open here. I have a big secret, you see. One that I'm finally ready to share.*

My brain has trouble with letters and associated sounds. Things can get jumbled and blend together all wrong. In school, I really struggled to read. Then, whenever I got stressed, I would freeze up. Zone out.

Think of a possum playing dead. Nothing to see here, folks!

Once I got my dyslexia diagnosis, things improved. I had a word and reason that explained my daily struggles, as well as tools to help me cope. After some hard work, I found my way out of that hole. Now I try to help others climb out of theirs. And guess what. Some of my Best Life Now clients have been dyslexic just like me.

But here's the kicker. The bare bones truth without a wrapper.

I never let any of them know. A part of me was still embarrassed. Ashamed. And yes, even scared.

I won't do that anymore.

So, what's this life coach's best advice?

When you feel like hiding away or flat-out giving up, remind yourself that none of us is perfect. Everyone is spectacularly unique. Then stand up, fill your lungs and shout from the rooftops.

If I want to be free, I need to be me!

* * *

Ajax and his team were finishing up for the afternoon when Hux walked into the stables.

"Another blistering win for this one last week," Hux said, eyeing Someone's Prince Charming's whiteboard chart. "Good job, son."

After making a note about feed, Ajax set down the pen. "Things are certainly getting back to normal."

Hux entered the stall to check Prince's hooves.

"I heard from Matt today," he said, rubbing a fingertip around one of the plates. "Paul Booshang finally came clean. Apparently over the years, he'd lost everything at the track. He said if he couldn't take down horse racing in its entirety, he wanted to at least cause a stir for some guys at the top. He had a personal gripe with Darnel…the way he'd treated his family…something about a tree house." Hux straightened. "Apparently a TV network has offered him a fortune for the story."

Ajax recalled one of Veda's arguments against the industry. "Losing your shirt… I wonder how many people can identify."

"Son, you can't help people like that. They have no control."

That's what Ajax had always thought, but that was kind of the point, wasn't it? "You have to admit we're at least part of the problem."

"We don't twist anyone's arm. We don't force anyone to get into bed with a loan shark."

Ajax paraphrased Veda. "A drug dealer doesn't force an addict to keep using, either."

Hux was on to the last hoof. "Hardly the same thing. Horse racing generates billions of dollars for the state's economy. It's a tradition." Joining Ajax again, Hux pushed on with another topic of conversation as he looked up and down the stalls. "So, update me on any new plans you have, partner."

Ajax had signed that contract. Half the land and half the profits were now his. A huge achievement, particularly knowing that he truly had his father's respect.

Only...he had thought it would feel better than this. That he might feel, well, really whole now. Complete.

"The new walker's almost finished," he said, grabbing his hat and heading to the door with Hux. "I put on another vet this morning. The very best credentials, and we're on the same page with regard to overmedicating."

All too often in the industry, horses were given powerful medications that allowed them to race despite their injuries.

Hux dropped his hat on his head. "Good. Good. We want a fair race."

"And healthy horses."

Hux's smile deepened as they headed out into the sunshine. "I'm so fortunate to have a son who wants nothing more than to carry on the family tradition. You've always been so dedicated. Such a natural."

Looking around the place, Ajax held his hat in his hands. "I've been at it a long time."

"And will be for a long time to come."

That had always been the plan, and Ajax hadn't

wanted anything more. Now... Well, he had other things on his mind, all to do with a strong-minded redhead who had put up a wall he couldn't find a way to break down.

"Something troubling you?" Hux asked. "Maybe something to do with Veda Darnel?"

Ajax tried to shrug it off. "I'm good."

Hux gave a thoughtful nod. "Well, you know what they say."

"No. What do they say?"

"Plenty more fish in the sea."

Ajax shut one eye as he winced. "I don't see Veda as a fish."

"I'm only saying that she must not be the one. But one day you'll find your special someone, no doubt about it. And when you do, you'll know. And so will she."

When Hux hailed a groom on his way to a tack room, Ajax headed back to the office with his father's words still ringing in his ears. Hux didn't know what he and Veda had discussed that day on Drake's porch. Her story was as private, and haunting, as they come. Ajax couldn't stop thinking about the circumstances surrounding her mom's death. That cowboy had been lower than a bottom-feeder. No wonder Veda had developed a lifelong aversion to that type.

But Ajax reassured himself again: he was nothing like that. He could never treat anyone that way. *Never*.

And yet those lines kept circling.

It's all in your head, darlin'.

I would never do that to you.

Yes, he had known a few women in his life, but as he had explained to Veda, he had never parted with anyone on bad terms. Fallon Kelly was a case in point. Except...

If he were to be 100 percent honest, he had always gotten out early for just that reason—to avoid the possibility of an ugly breakup. Put another way: he liked to have his cake and eat it, too. He wanted to enjoy the intimate company of a beautiful, engaging woman without the drag of making anything official.

But with Veda, that way of thinking—of feeling— just didn't seem to fit. Where she was concerned, the idea of commitment didn't spook him. In fact, he couldn't fathom a time when he didn't want to be with her, and only her.

Things had changed.

He had changed.

As Ajax reached the main paddock, Chester came trotting down from the house like he usually did this time of day. Trying to clear his head, Ajax deliberated on a chestnut prancing about, tossing her mane, while a buckskin colt capered up, his tail elevated and strong neck curved. Farther down, in the next paddock, two retired horses were grazing, stomping a hoof every now and then to shoo away flies. Over the years, he'd given away others to good and caring homes.

Scenes like this had filled and shaped his life. He'd grown up hankering for the next bustling day at the track. From a young age, he'd always leaped out of bed before the birds to start the day. The horses in his care had grade-A food and exercise, as well as the best grooms, riders, farriers and veterinary care.

He loved his horses. They were treated like kings.

But there were still injuries, some of them fatal. More than once he had watched, heartsick, as one of his own had gone down. The latest statistics said over fifty horses had died or been euthanized on New York State racecourses just this year.

He'd been one of the blinder-wearing crowd who argued that those numbers were built into the system. But what did that mean exactly? For the owners…for the horses…

Which side was he really on?

When Chester started wagging his tail, Ajax realized they had company. Susan was strolling over, a covered plate in her hand. He could smell the pie from here.

"Just pulled this out of the oven," she said, removing the cover to reveal a fat slice of his favorite: grape pie.

Ajax accepted the plate. "You're a honey, do you know that?"

Susan gave a big dimpled grin before she turned to study the horses.

"Sometimes I still can't believe I actually found my way here," she said. "This truly is my safe haven home."

Ajax had always believed this was his safe haven, too. That he would always feel rooted and cared for here. But lately trying to hold on to that had left a cold, heavy knot in his gut. He was hardly a kid anymore but still a long way from hanging up his reins. Was there more for him somewhere out there?

"You must be glad all that doping business is behind you," she said, leaning down to ruffle Chester's ears while his tail batted the ground. "And I'm so relieved that feud between Hux and Drake Darnel is finally over," she added. "Just goes to show. Differences can be worked out even when we might think there's no hope." She slid him a look. "I'm sure Veda would agree. She seems like a lovely girl."

"She is lovely. And smart." He paused, then added, "And strong."

"Yes, indeed," Susan said, looking out over the paddock again. "Diamonds are definitely out there. My ex-husband, however…well, he was a grimy lump of coal."

Ajax recalled that Veda's mother had stayed with Drake for the sake of the family. But Susan hadn't had children with her ex-husband. Why had she stayed so long? He hoped she wouldn't mind if he asked.

"Why didn't you leave the guy sooner?"

"Well, I married young. Taking those vows… I thought I had to stay. But over the years, of course the abuse wore me down, to the point I could barely think straight. Hux helped bring me back. I truly am a different person because of his love." She thought that through more and added, "Or maybe not different so much as… I think the right word is authentic. He's so lovely. And smart. And strong."

Ajax grinned. *Lovely. Smart. Strong.* Those words were a common link between Susan's love for Hux and his own thoughts on Veda. And Hux might have helped Susan, but she'd done just as much for him. Maybe more.

So, what would have happened to Hux, to their family, if Susan hadn't come along? Ajax wanted to believe that his father would have come out of that thick dark fog on his own. But he wondered....

And if *he* fell in love, married, had kids, and something happened to his wife—if she died... How would he deal? Would he cope or simply want to give in?

After Susan left with Chester bounding off ahead of her, Ajax took his pie into the office. As he sat behind his desk and opened his laptop, he mulled over Susan's words.

She had helped settle what he'd been struggling with for weeks. He needed to reach out to Veda again because he couldn't dance around the truth anymore. Earlier Hux had given sound advice about a person knowing when they had found their special someone. Ajax *did* know. He had to believe that Veda knew, too.

But he'd run out of things to say.

What could he do to convince her?

He set the pie aside to search Best Life Now. The link to Veda's website popped up. He checked out each page and ended up on her blog. The latest post had him riveted. He could literally hear her speaking to him, giving him advice.

If I want to be free, I need to be me.

Ajax thought back on those words the following weekend at the track. Someone's Prince Charming was two lengths ahead when he stumbled and broke down.

The examining veterinarian reported catastrophic fractures to both front ankles. The jockey, who had sustained serious injuries, was carried away on a stretcher. When the order was given to euthanize the horse, Ajax was there, kneeling at his friend's side.

On the drive home, his chest and eyes were burning so much, Ajax had to pull over. A bottle of Scotch kept him company through the night. By morning, he'd crossed that line and made up his mind.

To hell with anyone who didn't agree.

Sixteen

Veda heard it first from her dad.

The previous week when they'd talked on FaceTime, Drake had mentioned the "big news concerning the Rawsons." Veda had coughed out a laugh and told him point-blank he was wrong. But her father insisted; a Darnel farrier had confirmed the rumor just that day.

Ajax Rawson was no longer associated with Rawson Studs. No one knew for sure what big plans he had for himself, although talk was that he was still on the property working things through.

Veda hadn't spoken with Ajax since that day on her father's porch two whole months ago when she had opened up more about her past and made her position crystal clear. She had survived some tough breaks.

Now that she was in a good place, there was no turning back, only going forward.

At the time, Ajax had looked disappointed, but obviously he had accepted her decision and moved on. Of course, the breakup had brought her down. Coming out on her blog had helped build her sense of self up again, as did personally sharing her dyslexia experiences later with each of her clients. And if she ever felt like curling up into a ball, she reminded herself that she wouldn't feel this way forever. Over time, her love for Ajax would fade.

Unfortunately she couldn't see that happening anytime soon.

Before ending that FaceTime call, Drake had suggested she visit again. How about this weekend? She had smiled and said good idea. It felt weird actually looking forward to spending time with her dad. Even weirder to anticipate driving right past the Rawson property knowing that Ajax was probably still there.

Now, as she traveled on the interstate, getting closer to the Rawsons' connecting road, Veda told her heart to quit pumping so hard. But memories from the night her car had spun out were coming thick and fast. Ajax racing down through the rain to rescue her still felt like something out of a dream.

Her hands were damp on the steering wheel by the time the Rawsons' billboard-size sign came into view. Would things have been different between her and Ajax if that doping scandal hadn't hit? But of course, realistically, they were never going to make it. He had his life and, yes, she had hers.

Veda stepped on the accelerator and forced herself to look straight ahead. She was going to visit her father. When she arrived, Drake would welcome her with a smile and perhaps even a hug. Going through to the kitchen, he would brew his tea while she poured herself a wine. Then they would venture out to the same spot where she and Ajax had relaxed after he had driven her home from the hospital that day. She could see the tree house from there.

Veda slammed on the brakes and caught her breath as another *new* sign came into view.

Welcome to Giddy Up Safe Haven.

The letters were multicolored and cartoonish like the ones from that old birthday book. A drawing of a grinning horse, standing with his front legs crossed, made her smile even harder. Then she spotted something else in a corner. A blue bucket with a dog sitting up inside it. It was small and fluffy with apricot dots on each cheek.

A blasting horn sent Veda jumping out of her seat. As the flatbed truck swerved around her, she turned onto the shoulder of the entrance road. Her heart was slamming against her ribs, and she couldn't contain the grin because this was more than a coincidence.

The Rawsons owned hundreds of acres, including this hill. Ajax knew she had a dream of having a farm where animals didn't have to work or breed or die. A sanctuary. A safe haven. That puppy—little Gus in his bucket—was the bow that tied this all together.

Ajax had created Giddy Up Safe Haven, and he'd done it with her in mind.

Bubbling with excitement, she turned into the entrance road and drove to the crest of that hill. On the plateau, a freshly painted Cape Cod cabin appeared, as well as post-and-rail paddocks, a big old barn and then...

Well, suddenly all those warm, bubbly feelings began to pop and evaporate because on top of being a magnificent example of the male species, Veda knew the truth. Ajax was also a pro in the art of seduction. Lanie had said that he was all about the chase. And it had certainly been true where they were concerned. So, what was really going on here?

Braking, Veda saw movement up ahead. Three horses—a gray, a brindle and a cream—were trotting up to a fence. Ajax was holding two buckets, presumably full of feed. But beneath the wide brim of his black hat, his undivided attention was fixed on her approach.

A yearning, almost desperate heat filled Veda in an instant. In his white button-down, his shoulders looked even bigger. The vee below his open collar was definitely more bronzed. The weight of the buckets strained his gorgeous forearms, highlighting the corded muscle. She could imagine his crooning voice now, saying how beautiful she was, how good she smelled, how much he had missed her and...

"Well, dang, Veda baby. I knew you'd be back."

He had promoted a rumor that suggested he had given up the Rawson brand, his career and the prestige. But seriously? A couple of rescue horses and a rickety old cabin wouldn't hold his attention. That said, she was almost flattered that he'd gone to so much trouble to set up such an elaborate prop.

As he set down the buckets and sauntered over, rocking a pair of worn blue jeans like no other man could, Veda bit her lip to divert the pain that was filling her all the way to the top. He thought he could charm her, fool her, by using a dream she held so dear to her heart?

Setting her jaw, she threw open the car door.

Sorry, cowboy.

Guess again.

As Ajax dropped the buckets and headed over to the Best Life Now vehicle, his thumping heart nearly burst out of his chest. Veda must have seen the Giddy Up sign on her way to her father's place. Her showing up out of the blue gave this move a special seal of approval. He knew his mom was smiling down, cheering him on, giving her blessing.

Just as Hux had done when Ajax had explained why he needed to move on.

He had loved his life growing up. He would always hold dear memories of the farm through his years from a child to a man. But now more than ever, he knew he'd made the right choice. And as Veda got out of the car and her gaze meshed with his, it all felt so damn good, he broke into a jog.

Drawing closer, he watched the breeze play through her hair, making it dance while it pushed that summer dress against her body, emphasizing every delicious sweep and curve. Her green eyes were sparkling in the sunshine, and the beautiful lips he longed to taste again were…

Turned down?

Ajax pulled back.

Veda had found her way here but she wasn't happy? Surely it wasn't anything he could have done. Not this time. Perhaps she'd had another argument with Drake. Maybe there'd been bad news with regard to her business.

Well, if she was looking for a shoulder to lean on, two arms to bring her close and lift her up, she had come to the right place.

He picked up the pace again until he was running right at her. As he swept by, he grabbed her around the waist, hoisted her up against him and twirled her around. He felt her stiffen because of course she was caught off guard. And when he stopped spinning and let her slide down against him, he kept the surprises coming. As soon as her mouth was within range, he kissed her like he'd dreamed of doing every minute of every day since he'd let her walk away.

Now she was back.

You'd better believe she was here to stay.

Ajax worked the kiss, cupping the back of her head while he held her snug against him. Feeling her feet flap in the air, he pressed in deeper as every starving part of him hardened and cried out for more. Veda was gripping what she could of his shoulders, her fingers digging into his shirt while her lower half pressed against his belt. While working on this place these past weeks, he had routinely lost himself in daydreams about a reunion…how steamy and flat-out joyous the makeup sex would be. But this moment was about way more than anything physical. This connection was real, and no matter how many challenges the future threw their way, they would make it through together. To the depths of his soul, he knew that.

But then…

Well, something changed.

Veda didn't seem to be gripping his shirt so much as trying to shove him away. And while he was certain she'd been kissing him back a moment ago, now her mouth was closed, shutting him out.

Pulling back, he searched her eyes. They were shining with emotion. But he wouldn't call it love.

"Let me down!" She pushed him again. "What are you doing? Are you crazy?"

It took another second for those words to sink in. After setting her down, he tried to figure out how the hell he had read it so wrong.

"I get out of my car and you literally jump on me," she was saying. "You really have a problem, you know that?"

He blinked several times, rubbed his brow. "I presumed you were here to see me."

"I was curious," she said, rearranging her dress, which was askew after that amazing midair kiss.

His lips were still burning, begging for more. But he needed to stay focused and rewind to a time before he had believed she had actually wanted him to sweep her off her feet.

"Okay." Holding up both hands, he took in a deep breath, blew it out. "What's going on?"

"I was driving by," she explained, "when I saw the sign. I'd heard rumors."

"That I'd walked away from Rawsons. Correct."

Her eyes widened. "You really did?"

"I decided that I needed to do something different. Something where I could be around horses but..."

His words trailed off because this had all taken such a sharp turn in the wrong direction. What was she so pissed about? What had he done wrong now?

He threw a glance at the new paddock railings he'd put up, then at the cabin roof he'd almost finished repairing. The old barn was big enough to house twenty retired racehorses.

Veda was looking around, too, like she was waiting to be ambushed or expecting a big rock to crash on her head.

"You've really put a lot of work into this," she finally said, obviously remembering the pictures he'd shown her on his phone.

"Yeah." His mouth twisted as the backs of his eyes kind of prickled. "I did."

She crossed her arms. "But if this is all for me, you shouldn't have bothered."

He just looked at her now because...*wow*.

Just.

Wow.

"If you want to know, this wasn't just for you," he said over the god-awful lump in his throat. "It was for *us*. You were the one who said to go after the things that matter most. I thought I could make us both happy. In fact, when I set my mind to it, I felt so good, so sure, I thought you'd be blown away."

She hesitated, then said, "You really thought that I'd trust you?"

"Right." He stepped back into her space. "Because if this is going to work, and I know that it can, we need to trust each other. That's what love is about, damn it!"

He clenched his jaw and dialed it back. She obviously wasn't ready for this. Would she ever be?

Raking a hand through his hair, he groaned. "I need to shut up now—"

"No," she said as quick as a whip. Then the corners of her mouth twitched. It wasn't exactly a smile but not an outright scowl, either.

He tried to corral the emotions needing to break free. But he couldn't contain the way he felt about her. Right now, this minute, he needed her to know it all.

"I enrolled in college. A bachelor's degree in animal biology. Vet school is another four years at least on top of that, so maybe not—"

"Maybe *yes*." She came forward. "That's so amazing. You always wanted to do that."

Ajax remembered the day when Someone's Prince Charming had broken down. He hadn't been able to save him. But he'd made his decision very soon after that.

"And I took some advice from your blog," he said.

Her eyes widened. "You read my blog?"

"I've done way more than that." He let it all out. "I've fallen in love with you, Veda. But it's more than that, too." He held her arms. "I know I want to spend the rest of my days with you."

When her lips quivered with a growing smile and her eyes filled with what he hoped were happy tears, he looped his arms around her waist and tugged her close again.

"I've brought over my retirees," he said, flickering a glance at the trio. "There'll be more to come. And there's plenty of room for pet pigs and sheep and a fluffy little dog we'll call Gus, too."

She still wasn't talking. Not a croak. Not a peep.

But the tears in her eyes were close to falling, and her lips were definitely calling to him again. So he leaned that bit closer, held her that much tighter and laid out the last of his speech.

"This is who I am," he told her. "This is who I want to be. With you every damn day for as long as we live."

This time when they kissed, Ajax felt a sense of certainty spiral through him, filling him up in a way that reaffirmed what he already knew. He had made the right choice. Veda would always be his sweetheart.

Veda was "the one."

When he slowly broke the kiss, her eyes were heavy with the same wonderful emotions he was feeling.

"Veda," he said, "you are the best thing that's ever happened to me."

"You really mean that? The *best*?"

She looked too choked up to get more words out. But then she took a breath, and asked in a near whisper, "Ajax?"

He smiled and brought her closer. "Yes, Veda."

"I love you, too. I'm pretty sure I loved you from the start."

Then he was kissing her again, lifting her higher, loving her even more. And he knew this time they had done it.

Theirs would be the best life ever.

The best there ever was.

* * * * *

*Don't miss a single story in
the About That Night... duet:*

The Case for Temptation
One Night with His Rival

by Robyn Grady

*Available exclusively
from Harlequin Desire!*

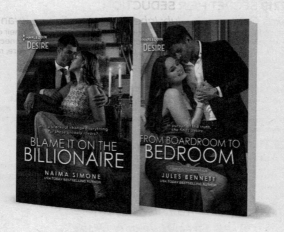

COMING NEXT MONTH FROM

DESIRE

Available March 3, 2020

#2719 SECRET HEIR SEDUCTION
Texas Cattleman's Club: Inheritance • by Reese Ryan
Fashion mogul Darius Taylor-Pratt is shocked to learn he's the secret heir of the wealthy Blackwood family! That's not the only surprise as he reconnects with his ex, diamond heiress Audra Lee Covington. As old passions flare, new revelations threaten everything...

#2720 HEARTBREAKER
Dynasties: Mesa Falls • by Joanne Rock
Gage Striker vows to protect Mesa Falls Ranch from prying paparazzi at any cost—even when the press includes his former lover, Elena Rollins. Past misunderstandings fuel current tempers, but will this fire between them reignite their attraction?

#2721 JET SET CONFESSIONS
by Maureen Child
Fiona Jordan is a professional fixer and her latest job is bringing billionaire Luke Barrett back to his family business. As she goes undercover, the sparks between them are instant and undeniable. But she learns not everything is easy to fix when Luke discovers her true identity...

#2722 RECLAIMING HIS LEGACY
Louisiana Legacies • by Dani Wade
Playboy Blake Boudreaux will do anything to protect his family...including seducing the beautiful philanthropist Madison Armantine to get back a beloved heirloom. But as the secrets—and desire—between them grow, he'll have to reveal the truth or lose her forever...

#2723 ONE NIGHT WITH HIS RIVAL
About That Night... • by Robyn Grady
After a night of passion, smooth-talking cowboy Ajax Rawson and successful life coach Veda Darnel don't expect it to happen again...until it does. But will old family business rivalries threaten to end their star-crossed romance before it even begins?

#2724 THE DATING DARE
Gambling Men • by Barbara Dunlop
Jilted by their former lovers, friends James Gillen and Natasha Remington vow to reinvent themselves and maybe find love again in the process. But their daring new makeovers reveal a white-hot attraction neither was expecting...

YOU CAN FIND MORE INFORMATION ON UPCOMING HARLEQUIN TITLES, FREE EXCERPTS AND MORE AT HARLEQUIN.COM.

HDCNM0220

When billionaire bad boy Mercury Steele discovers his car is stolen, he's even more shocked to find out who's in the driver's seat—the mysterious beauty Sloan Donahue. As desire and secrets build between them, has this Steele man finally met his match?

Read on for a sneak peek at
Seduced by a Steele
by New York Times *bestselling author Brenda Jackson.*

"So, as you can see, my father will stop at nothing to get what he wants. He doesn't care who he hurts or maligns in the process. I refuse to let your family become involved."

A frown settled on his face. "That's not your decision to make."

"What do you mean it's not my decision to make?"

"The Steeles can take care of ourselves."

"But you don't know my father."

"Wrong. Your father doesn't know us."

Mercury wondered if anyone had ever told Sloan how cute she looked when she became angry. How her brows slashed together over her forehead and how the pupils of her eyes became a turbulent dark gray. Then there was the way her chin lifted and her lips formed into a decadent pout. Observing her lips made him remember their taste and how the memory had kept him up most of the night.

"I don't need you to take care of me."

Her words were snapped out in a vicious tone. He drew in a deep breath. He didn't need this. Especially from her and definitely not this morning. He'd forgotten to cancel his date last night with

Raquel and she had called first thing this morning letting him know she hadn't appreciated it. It had put him in a bad mood, but, unfortunately, Raquel was the least of his worries.

"You don't?" he asked, trying to maintain a calm voice when more than anything he wanted to snap back. "Was it not my stolen car you were driving?"

"Yes, but—"

"Were you not with me when you discovered you were being evicted?" he quickly asked, determined not to let her get a word in, other than the one he wanted to hear.

"Yes, but—"

"Did I not take you to my parents' home? Did you not spend the night there?"

Her frown deepened. "Has anyone ever told you how rude you are? You're cutting me off deliberately, Mercury."

"Just answer, please."

She didn't say anything and then she lifted her chin a little higher, letting him know just how upset she was when she said, "Yes, but that doesn't give you the right to think you can control me."

Control her? Was that what she thought? Was that what her rotten attitude was about? Well, she could certainly wipe that notion from her mind. He bedded women, not controlled them.

"Let me assure you, Sloan Donahue, controlling you is the last thing I want to do to you." There was no need to tell her that what he wouldn't mind doing was kissing some sense into her again.

Don't miss what happens next in
Seduced by a Steele
by Brenda Jackson, part of her Forged of Steele series!

Available April 2020 wherever
Harlequin Desire books and ebooks are sold.

Harlequin.com

SPECIAL EXCERPT FROM

HQN

When India Robidoux needs help with her brother's high-profile political campaign, she has no choice but to face the one man she's been running away from for years—Travis, her sister's ex-husband. One hot summer night when Travis was still free, they celebrated her birthday with whiskey and an unforgettable kiss. The memory is as strong as ever—and so are the feelings she's tried so hard to forget…

Read on for a sneak peek of
Forbidden Promises *by Synithia Williams*

"We need everyone else in the family to demonstrate that family and friendships are still strong despite the divorce. I'm pairing Travis up with Byron and India."

India's jaw dropped. Everyone turned to her. Everyone except Elaina, who stood even more rigid next to the window.

"Me? Why me?" The words came out in a weird croak and she cleared her throat.

"Because you make sense," Roy explained.

Travis crossed the room to the food. India quickly stepped out of his way. Her hip bumped the table, rattling the platters set on the surface. Travis raised an eyebrow. She forced herself to relax and nod congenially. She wasn't supposed to react when he was near. They were cool now. They'd cleared the air. Deemed what had happened years ago a mistake. She couldn't run and hide when he came near.

She focused on Roy. "What do I have to do?"

"There will be a few times when we'll need family members to campaign for Byron if he can't be there personally. We've got a lot of ground to cover, and if we can show a united front, I'd recommend having at least two family members together in those cases. I'll partner you with Travis for those appearances. The two of you can play up how great he is as a brother and friend."

Roy made it all sound so easy. Sure, everything seemed simple to everyone else. They didn't realize the easy friendship she'd once shared with Travis was gone. No one knew she could barely look at him without thinking about how she'd loved him. How she'd dreamed about his kiss even after he'd married Elaina. Fought to forget the feel of his hands on her body as she'd stood next to her sister at their wedding.

"Now that that's settled," Roy said, obviously taking India's silence as agreement, "we can get to the next point."

"Are you okay with spending time with me?" Travis asked in a low voice.

India's heart did a triple beat. He'd slid close to her as Roy moved on. His proximity was like an electric current vibrating against her skin.

"Of course," she said quickly. "Why wouldn't I be?"

"You wouldn't be the only person not wanting my company lately."

The disappointment in his voice made her look up. He wasn't looking at her. He frowned at the floor. His lips were pressed into a tight line. She wanted to reach out and touch him. To attempt to erase the sadness from his features. "I'll always want your company."

His head snapped up and he studied her face. She really shouldn't have said that. The words were too close to how she really felt.

"We'll need to pick out a suitable fiancée for him."

Roy's voice and the randomness of his words broke India from the captivating hold of Travis's eyes. She tuned back into the conversation. "Fiancée? Who needs a fiancée?"

Byron chuckled and placed a hand on his chest. "I do."

India looked from her father to Byron. Were they serious? "You didn't mention you were getting married."

Byron shrugged as if not mentioning a possible fiancée wasn't a huge deal. "I didn't decide to ask her until recently. We've been dating for a few months."

Dating for a few months? Wasn't he the same guy Travis had teased about three women calling him just yesterday? Her brother was a ladies' man, but he wasn't a dog. He wouldn't be considering marriage to someone if he still had multiple women calling his phone. Would he? Had he changed that much while she'd been gone?

She spun toward Travis. "You aren't letting him do this, are you?" She pointed over her shoulder at her brother.

Travis stilled with a chocolate croissant halfway to his mouth. "Do what?"

She stepped closer and lowered her voice. "Marry this Yolanda person. Who is she? Are they really dating?"

Travis sighed. "They've gone back and forth for a while."

Which really meant that her brother had been sleeping with her for a few months, but there was no commitment. Her hands balled into fists. She couldn't believe this!

"Don't spout off the campaign bullshit with me," she said in a low voice that wouldn't carry to her plotting relatives still in the room. "Not with me. This is a campaign maneuver."

"Roy has a point." Travis said the words slowly, as if he couldn't believe he was agreeing with Roy. "Your brother can't be a senator if he's out there picking up women in bars. He's got to settle down. Yolanda is who he chose."

"Did he choose her?" She wouldn't doubt that Roy, or their dad, picked the perfect woman for him.

"He said he chose her."

"Do you believe him?"

Travis glanced at the group huddled together. "I want to believe him. Giving up what you want for an unhappy marriage isn't worth the price of a senate seat." He turned a heavy gaze on her. "Not when it ruins a true chance at happiness."

India leaned back. She was stunned into silence. Her throat was dry and her stomach fell to her feet. The regret in his eyes created a deep ache in her chest. Had he given up something for an unhappy marriage? Before the words could spill from her lips, he took a bite of the croissant and strolled over to join the strategizing team, leaving India with another unanswered question to taunt her at night.

Don't miss what happens next in
Forbidden Promises by Synithia Williams!
Available February 2020 wherever
HQN books and ebooks are sold.

HQNBooks.com